A Marquess of Roses

An English Garden

Steffy Smith

A feisty hoyden. A devilish rake.
Step back in time to Regency London.
The ton is is ready for another season
to start but is the ton ready for
Lady Charlotte FitzHugh of Kentwell?
The Marquess of Sunderland, Adam Langdon,
will not know what hits him when he sets
his emerald eyes upon her amethyst orbs.
Nor will the Lord whose foot she stamps on.
Nor the Viscount she knee's in the bollocks.
No shrinking violet is Lady Charlotte, and
the Marquess will be unable to resist.

Dedication

To the loved ones reading this that supported me on this journey – I thank you all and you each know exactly who you are.

Prologue

Kent House, Grosvenor Square, 1829

The Duke of Kentwell, Lord Ernest Fitzroy, had become known as the ton's most intriguing recluse and enigma. Recluse may not be the best description as he always attended his parliament obligations, stayed involved in his charitable works and, on occasion, accepted social invites from the few friends he held close. The Duke of Kentwell had not always been this way. Many remembered his vibrancy and love of social gatherings. For, you see, Kentwell, as he was commonly known, had been married to a diamond of the first water of the 1806 season. And it was no secret that this marriage was one of true love and not convenience, monetary gain, or political alliance, as were so many other ton marriages. Kentwell and his wife, his Duchess Elizabeth, lived an idyllic and charmed life, welcoming their only child, a daughter Charlotte, in 1809. She was a mirror image of his Elizabeth. Despite never conceiving again, both parents were content. So content

1

that he named Charlotte the heir to his fortune and any future son she bore heir to the dukedom.

Their perfect world was torn to pieces in 1817. While on the way home from the Opera, a carriage accident claimed the life of his beloved Elizabeth. Kentwell, seriously injured himself, still held on to Elizabeth's lifeless form until passers-by gently took her from his grasp to attend to his injuries. The driver was also pronounced dead at the scene and those who attended his body could smell the most probable cause of this tragedy: alcohol. A cheap whiskey rolled off the young man in strong fumes. It was lucky for the deceased that his body had already been carted away and buried when Kentwell found out a few days later. It was clear to everyone that he would surely have killed the driver all over again.

The duke entered a mourning period with Charlotte, who was only 8 years old, and closed off his home and his life from society for the next 12 years, until Charlotte turned twenty. The only people Charlotte dealt with were the servants who had been loyal to Kentwell Manor for generations, her handpicked tutors, paid handsomely for their discretion, the townspeople in Kentwell and his sister, Aunt Anne, who doted on Charlotte as a surrogate mother figure. He had raised his daughter to be strong, wise and, perhaps, a tiny bit wilful. He could not be prouder.

When invites were sent out to the ton, after 12 years of silence, the invitations were torn open with haste and gasps of shocks, followed with curious murmurs and speculation. Kentwell was inviting anyone who was anyone to his London townhouse, Kent House, in Grosvenor Square for Charlotte's formal debut into society. Kent House had not hosted an event in over a decade! The ton tittered and buzzed as rumours circulated about why Kentwell had kept her hidden away and why he had now decided to enter back into society. Was it because the Lady Charlotte had grown unsightly in looks or weight? Or was she an embarrassment of some kind? Or had she simply gone mad with grief from losing her mother? The rational people, who could still recall vague memories of Charlotte in childhood, remembered a beautiful child who was a miniature of her mother. The truth was that it was none of those reasons. He had simply mourned longer than he intended and, once his grief had passed, he was not ready to lose his daughter, to a life of her own. He knew this was selfish and his clever and beautiful child needed to be able to lead her own life. In saying this, he had no intention in explaining himself to his fellow judgemental peers. They would learn soon enough.

The ton did not need any explanation. They were content with their gossip. The social set loved nothing more than an excuse to be judgemental. The more reasonable people of the ton just assumed he was overprotective from losing his duchess but, nonetheless, they still held mild suspicions that there was something slightly odd indeed. Most young ladies debuted between 16 and 18 and everyone knew it was a downhill slope to spinsterhood for ladies in their twenties. Those of the ton who secured invites all eagerly responded in the affirmative for their families, including the sons of marriageable age, forced to attend as, unattractive or not, the dowry would surely be of enormous proportions. Enough to appease any vain concerns. As the staff at Kent House attempted to keep up with the swarm of replies and preparations to open the house for the season, the host in question sat with his head in his hands. It was time to introduce Lady Charlotte to society.

Chapter One

Gazing outside her bedroom window at Kent House, Lady Charlotte took in the sights of the rose garden, which was identical to her garden at Kentwell Manor. The roses, all shades of pink, red and white, were cultivated and tended to in memory of her mother by the gardeners and Charlotte herself. She adored roses, their scent and delicate beauty along with the nostalgia they created of her mother. Despite living in the country all these many years away from society, she never felt lonely. All the people that encompassed her daily life showered her with love and attention. Even though she would always miss her mother, she could honestly say she never lacked maternal attention, in the guise of Aunt Anne.

However, her upcoming season debut was causing her to frown with worry. She couldn't bear the thought of seeking out marriage and being plucked away from all she had ever known.

As usual, her aunt's voice popped into her head: *Ladies do not frown.*

Lost in her own thoughts, she flung herself on the bed in

"

what she knew was a most unladylike manner. The thought of being married to a strange man and having to live in his strange house brought on a feeling of misery she was not accustomed to. Sighing, she knew she had to resign herself to this fate, 'twas her duty to marry and provide heirs, not only to her husband but for her own estates.

She needed to marry and birth a son so he may inherit the dukedom, or it would pass to the next male relative. Actually, she thought, she needed two sons, one to also inherit the title of her future husband. 'So much pressure,' she grumbled to herself. She held few memories of any people she might have met: the friends and peers of her parents and their offspring. She did recall another heir to a dukedom, Portsmouth, who had purportedly turned into a rake of large proportions – if the gossip that had trickled back to the country could be believed. She was only a little concerned about any shortcomings she may have once in society, being away for so long. But she did not fault her father, as she would not trade her upbringing for another, as unconventional as it might have been.

As she gazed around her room in Kent House, not as large but just as grand, she noted the walls were papered in a soft floral lilac print and the wooden panelling was a light brown that matched the furniture. Her favourite spot was a large bay window positioned to allow natural light to brighten the room. She realised that, even though she was as educated as any man, just as accomplished a rider and a perfect shot with a pistol, she was still a woman and needed to take her place as a Lady and do ladylike things. That is what a husband would expect. Aunt Anne had covered all the necessary etiquette lessons, so she knew how to deliver these expectations, but it was just that she enjoyed other pursuits as well.

The perfect way to describe me, she thought, *is a hoyden.* "The least ideal adjective for society ideals," she giggled to herself.

From what she did understand about ladies of the ton, they wore silly smiles for men, instead of impressing upon them intelligent conversation, and enjoyed gossip. And all the simpering and frippery that went on only caused her to roll her eyes – another unladylike habit Aunt Anne frequently admonished her for.

"A lady does not roll her eyes."

The guidance she received from Aunt Anne was that many of the men amongst the peerage did not care for a female opinion and she should take her time during the season to find someone suitable who would. She knew she was lucky, as ladies didn't normally get the option to do so. Aunt Anne explained that, unlike her loud entrance to every room she entered, the women tended to be demure, and she could not help but find this information amusing. She kept up with the gossip and knew they were anything but demure for all their outward ladylike behaviour!

Macy, her maid, had a sister who worked for a Countess who was always inviting her friends over to gossip. Macy's sister overheard this gossip, which then made its way back to her so she could note down any useful tidbits to help her understand the ways of society. She had stopped being shocked a long time ago with the debauchery that went on in the ton, the scandalous affairs, the innocent misses who smiled shyly behind fans but engaged in clandestine meetings in the gardens.

Taking stock of herself, she knew that she would not be one of those wives to turn a blind eye to such blatant affairs, which, according to Macy, was a norm in many of these marriages. And marrying also meant participating in the physical intimacy that seemed to be the cause of all the debauchery. Not that she was naïve. She knew some of the facts of life, having even seen animals on the estate engage in such copulation. Once, she even came upon two servants. Her face flushed at the memory, recalling how she had kept herself hidden and watched as the maid and groom kissed and touched each other's bodies. They had undressed each other till the maid's breasts were exposed and his erection was out of his breeches. She watched the groom lift the maid's skirts. She saw how they both moved in pleasure, their moans telling her as such. Charlotte kept watching till the very end when she heard the maid shriek and the groom shudder until they just stood there panting. This voyeurism had left her warm in her own innocent body; her own breathing had grown heavy.

"I truly am not cut out to be a lady," she mumbled. "I think like a man."

A knock at the door broke into her thoughts. "How are you settling in, Dearest?" Aunt Anne asked, her smiling face entering the room.

"Very well! I have just been thinking about the season, the future."

"Are you worried?" Her Aunt's face wrinkled in concern.

"Yes and no. I think I am more eager to find myself some friends instead of a husband," she said, flopping on the other side of the bed. Anne gave an indulgent laugh. How she loved her niece's spirit.

"I predict you will find both and will keep us very busy with your social calendar." She turned to leave. "Oh, and Charlotte, *ladies do not flop all over the bed*," she admonished, unable to hold back her smile.

The Marquess of Sunderland and heir to the Duke of Portsmouth, Adam Langdon, or Langdon as most called him, stood up over the woman he had just finished pleasuring from behind and caught his breath. This was his preferred position in situations like this, as he could tell that the widow, Lady Adele, was forming an attachment, not an emotional one but a possessive one. She wanted more than the dalliance he was prepared to offer. The less eye contact he made, well, the better in his mind. In hindsight, he should have made an excuse to leave rather than take up her sexual favours but, as per usual, he chose to be reckless in his personal pursuits. He knew he made reckless gambles, participated in reckless races, and so, naturally, he was quite reckless in his sexual exploits. He genuinely enjoyed giving a woman pleasure and having that pleasure returned. He had learned many tricks from the most skilled courtesans, which was another reason he was a sought-out lover.

His saving grace was that he always came out on top and never mixed pleasure with business. He was very shrewd and proficient when it came to the management of his estates.

It also did not hurt that he was one of the most handsome men amongst the peerage who would inherit a dukedom, he thought, staring into a mirror as he fixed his cravat. It was not at all surprising that he always had women on his tail. And he loved women. He did not care if the woman was widowed, married or a courtesan. He would leave them all satisfied, as long as they knew to expect no obligations from him. The only females he would not dally with were virgins. He shuddered at the thought. Not only was this dangerous territory but they also acted like insipid little dolls, battering their lashes and hanging on to his every word while they plotted how to best set their marriage traps. Little did they know it would be a cold day in hell before he was tricked into a compromising position. He realised he was jaded when it came to the concept of love and, from all his many dalliances, it became apparent that 'love' was a rarity. He did not care to love or be loved. Aside from his parents and very few couples he knew, love matches were rare, and he had no interest in finding one, just a suitable woman to bear and raise his heirs. When the time was right.

During his musings while he dressed, he realised Adele had been talking and caught the end of her sentence, "... going to the Kentwell soirée". Frowning, he recalled his father had informed him of a ball he must attend tomorrow. He only held brief recollections of Kentwell, who his father knew from parliament, but otherwise was aware Kentwell did not attend social engagements. A brief memory stirred that his mother was acquainted with his deceased wife and Adam had a brief memory of an argumentative little girl. Adele prattled on, citing all the rumours currently circulating about Charlotte.

Adam shrugged, fighting the urge to roll his eyes at the rumours. He did not recall anything wrong with the child nor had his father ever mentioned as such – just that old Kentwell was very proud of his daughter's intelligence. Curious that he did not mention grace nor beauty but no matter. Whatever dowry Kentwell put up, unsightly or not, she would have a steady stream of offers he mused. It was no secret many men of the peerage, whilst holding impressive titles, sometimes held quite unimpressive wealth. As Adam picked up his walking stick and top hat and turned to farewell Adele, she pounced on to his right side, hugging him close, and asked if he would be her escort to the ball.

Shaking his head, he cursed his reckless impulses, regretting dallying with her. Gently he removed her body from his and advised he would be attending with his parents. Kissing her cheek, he headed for the door but could feel her eyes boring into his back with just enough force to highlight her fury. Sighing as he bid good day to her servants, he exited her townhouse and inhaled a deep breath of fresh air to clear his lungs of the strong perfume Adele liked to douse herself in. He hailed a hackney to take him to his gentlemen's club, Whites, where his three best friends awaited him.

Adam entered the comfort of Whites and found his best friends waiting for him: the Earl of Chester, Lucas Belmont, Viscount Anthony Whitby, and Baron Jeremy Dunbar. Adam smiled with genuine affection and he studied them as he approached, noting how they had matured since reaching their mid-twenties. *Well, somewhat*, he thought wryly. Their friendship hailed back to their boyhood days at Eton and then as young men at Oxford. They even completed their tour abroad together before coming back to London and tearing up the ton. As he sat down and poured himself a brandy from the crystal bottle on the table, it was Jeremy who spoke first, grinning as he blew out a ring of cigar smoke.

"I smell sex and a cloying parfum. Shall I presume to say you just came from serving one Lady Adele?"

Adam punched him lightly in the shoulder and sighed.

"Yes, to my chagrin. I should have quit before I sunk myself deeper. I almost did not make it out. She actually wanted me to escort her to the ball tomorrow night. Like I would fall for that sly attempt to lay claim to me in a public setting."

His friends all laughed and informed him of what he had missed out on. There were new wagers on the betting book regarding the Kentwell Ball and his chit and rumours circulating that she was not comely nor overweight and of whom the top three gentlemen were that would most likely court her, since they were in most need of a rich dowry and desperate to wed. Adam felt a pang of guilt as he chuckled with his friends, pondering why the ton always felt the need to gossip at the potential misfortunes of others.

"Why do you think Kentwell kept her away from society for so long?" Jeremy asked.

"It is odd. She should have had a season or two by now," said Anthony.

"I don't think there is any unusual reason," Adam shrugged. "I imagine grief does funny things to a man." Everyone knew how distraught Kentwell had been when he had lost his wife.

"In my opinion, raising a child away from the ton may not be such a bad thing. I barely held one conversation last year that did not revolve around shopping, gossip or marriage hints." Lucas added, resulting in a chorus of 'hear, hear' from Jeremy and Anthony.

"I wouldn't know, my good men. As you all know, I make it a point to never dance with a chit out on a season." Anthony threw a cigar butt at him, as they all laughed.

He had another uncomfortable thought, *What if Kentwell heard about this? His parents would be unimpressed.*

Chapter One

After voicing his concern, Jeremy advised him that Kentwell had cancelled his membership years ago and the bets were circling around the younger men. He relaxed and sat back to catch up with his friends. Lucas was in between mistresses and wondering if it was time he looked for a bride. Anthony was tight lipped about his personal life and said he had things on his mind other than amusing himself between a woman's thighs, including a poor harvest. Jeremy was fighting with his current mistress, who was becoming greedier and more demanding. He nodded in sympathy with his friends, knowing how damaging a poor yield can be and how exhausting a woman could be.

They agreed to meet tomorrow night at the ball, to stay out of reach of any potential match making, and to enjoy the drinks and merriment before heading to a card game at a less reputable event. Adam could hear the men at White's talking about the bets and the upcoming ball and truly hoped it would be a sound affair. As sorry as he was starting to feel for her, he, for one, was not willing to be the sacrificial lamb to what could only be a husband hunt. With such a rich and full life, he had no need for the passing fancy of love or to be any lady's knight in shining armour.

Chapter Two

Organised chaos ran rampant in Kent House. The day of the ball had arrived. Charlotte, though schooled in how to host such an event, had never had an opportunity for hands-on experience. She was exhilarated and only a touch overwhelmed with the work to be done. Throwing herself into the task, she worked as hard as any servant until Aunt Anne called her away, advising she needed to begin readying herself. Pleased with all she had accomplished, she placed the final touches on the flower arrangements she had prepared to decorate the ballroom. The fresh, fragrant flowers would leave a pleasant smell throughout the room.

As she sat in her bath with her rose-scented oil, she realised keeping busy all day had kept her from focusing on the actual ball. Now, as she sat there alone with her thoughts, her trepidation began.

Will anyone remember me? Will they find me strange after all these years of seclusion? Will I make friends or are the social groups so well formed that there will be no opening for a newcomer?

As she sat there gnawing her bottom lip, Aunt Anne

came and scolded her, "Ladies do not chew on their lip." She gestured for her to get up. Deciding she would not allow inconsequential insecurities to control her mind, she stood up and looked to her Aunt, who was still talking.

"Come now, Charlotte. Let's dry you off, before you wrinkle, and work on styling your hair. Macy has the latest styles. Then we can get you dressed."

Rolling her eyes in affection, she stood up.

"Heaven forbid I wear my hair in last season's style."

Standing up into the towel Aunt Anne held for her, she looked into her Aunt's warm brown eyes and felt a wave of sadness at the thought of losing her companionship upon marriage. For so long, it had just been father, herself and Aunt Anne.

As Macy worked on her hair, Charlotte stared at her reflection, her thoughts wandering off to her appearance and what people would see. Her reflection stared back at her with her thick, glossy, dark chestnut-brown hair, which, under light, had golden strands. She saw sun-kissed skin from her time spent outdoors but she was still fair. She had high-sculpted cheekbones, her lips were full and pink and her teeth white and straight. She stared into her own eyes. They were like her mother's, open set and round, tinged with long, sooty-black lashes, and her irises were a vivid violet. She considered her eyes to be her best feature. Her hair complete in an elegant chignon, she stood up and removed her robe, again staring back at her almost naked reflection. The same fair glowing skin, rounded hips. Her breasts, she felt, were over large for her slim frame, but Macy had told her once, laughing, that they would make a man happy. Blushing at what Macy had alluded to, she tried to reign in her wayward thoughts.

They moved to her father and how he must be feeling.

She remembered how sad he had looked when he informed her it was time he introduced her to society. It made her determined to make her season a success. So he would have no regrets. Smiling to herself, she pictured her father being a doting grandfather, believing it to be the balm his heart needed. Aunt Anne had been watching her and saw the soft smile on her face. Beaming, she clutched her hands together, tears springing to her eyes.

"My darling girl, your smile is going to be the light of the season. You look gorgeous, just like your mother. Another diamond of the first water you will be."

"I hope I make mother, father and you proud," she said in her clear, strong voice.

She began to dress, first her chemise, her stays and stockings. And finally, her ball dress, the empire gown designed to flatter her figure, cinched at the waist and with a modest neckline. Taking one last look in the mirror at the lilac and white combination of silk, lace and tulle, she stepped forward to her Aunt, who adorned her with her mother's amethyst jewellery set. The precious gemstones glittering under the light were an eye-catching beauty. She fingered the gems, wishing she could have her mother's guidance this night.

She heard guests arriving, the butler announcing each appearance. From this distance, she could not hear the names but knew the ton was slowly filling the ballroom downstairs. Aunt Anne left to go attend to the guests. Her father's instructions were to wait until he sent Anne for her, as he wanted to debut her once everyone had arrived. Charlotte sat hands clasped tightly in her lap with Macy listening to her gossip while the butterflies danced in her stomach.

Chapter Two

Adam stood with his parents and friends in the ballroom of Kent House looking around at all the members of the peerage. It was a very crowded affair, but he could smell fresh flowers. He had dressed as the occasion befitted, wearing a deep green waist coat over a white shirt and a black tailcoat that was expertly tailored to his muscular frame. His cravat was tied around his neck, even though he found it stifling in these settings. He could never loosen it in the casual way he preferred when he was playing cards or drinking at a place of less repute. Instead of the preferred fashion of the dandies of his class with the intricate knots or the collars lifted high towards their ears, he just tied it with a simple respectable knot at the front.

Observing Kent House, he noted it was one of the larger townhouses, the furniture, and decorative pieces original and opulent. Servants, in their gold and white livery, brought expensive food and alcohol to the guests. Their livery matched the golden drapes that decorated the walls, shimmering under the bright lights of the enormous chandelier that descended from the middle of the ceiling. It was evident that no expense had been spared for this highly anticipated occasion. Kentwell himself had stood a few minutes with them talking, before being whisked away on host duties. Adam noted that Kentwell appeared jovial and not apprehensive and again he hoped the titterings he heard in the crowd were not carried back to him. Adam could clearly hear all the idle chatter and gossip around him, as everyone wondered when the Lady Charlotte would make her appearance.

His mother, the Duchess Lydia, turned to him and his friends and lifted a brow.

"You rogues are sticking awfully close tonight? Safety in numbers from the marriageable ladies?" His friends laughed with good humour at his mother's jibe.

"Ahh, your grace, we would not trade your presence for any of these lasses, if only you were still on the marriage mart," winked Jeremy, shamelessly. Adam gave him a joking punch in the arm as they all laughed.

"The gossip is rife tonight. I, for one, am appalled at this behaviour. I remember little Charlotte and she was the image of her mother and bright as well," said the Duchess, her tone now disgruntled.

Adam watched his mother, who was usually so stately in public, leaving her directness at home. He bought into his curiosity and asked why she was so bothered.

"I was good friends with Charlotte's mother; however, we slowly drifted apart when she married and, after she passed, I quarrelled with Kentwell, effectively removing any chance I had to see Charlotte grow up."

Adam listened to his mother's sad tone and was unsure what to say so decided to speak plainly. "I do not understand why he kept her tucked away all these years. How does he expect her just to come out into society after being kept sheltered for so long? The ton can be, no, is a cruel place."

"I suppose, my dear boy, the Duke, in his grief, was not rational for some time and maybe, once it started to pass, he did not know how to bring the poor poppet out. But do not fret. If she is anything like her mother, I imagine she has a strong and wild free spirit to not let anything, or anyone, get her down!"

Hearing his mother's mood brighten, he drew his attention back to the ball and the sad mood was soon forgotten. The duchess found a group of her friends and left the gentlemen to their devices. Finding themselves alone, their talk turned tawdry and they bantered freely.

They were on their third round of drinks, an hour or so into the party, and still waiting to see the Lady Charlotte. Adam didn't know why he was eager to see her, but he instinctively knew she would have grown into a beauty. He saw his father having an animated conversation with his parliament cronies and wondered what they were discussing. It was due to this that he did not notice Adele sidle her way between him and Jeremy, placing her arm in the crook of his elbow. His friends bowed and greeted her; however, he coolly welcomed her, wondering how he could make it clear this liaison would go no further.

"I have been looking for you," she purred in his ear. "I have saved the first waltz of the evening for you."

Ignoring the amusement on his friends' faces, he fought the urge to yank his arm back.

"Sorry but I am not feeling up to dancing tonight. Another time perhaps."

Despite the obvious rejection, she was undeterred and whispered, "Maybe you will be feeling up to something else tonight instead." She clearly hoped the lewd innuendo would pique his interest. Smothering a sigh, he saw she was not taking the hint.

Looking across the room, he caught the eye of Lady Isabel Pembroke, the wife of old Earl Pembroke, many years her senior. She had been seeking him out for a dalliance for a while now. He saw Adele had followed his line of sight. Her own eyes narrowed and, just as he went to disengage his arm and tell her he had a friend to greet, Kentwell appeared on the top of the ballroom stairs and called a hush.

"My dear guests, I welcome you to my home and thank you for celebrating and witnessing my beloved daughter, Lady Charlotte, come into her first season. Without further ado, as I hear many of you are awaiting with bated breath, let me present Lady Charlotte."

Two things registered in Adam's mind at that moment, one was the crowd's abashed grumbling of being caught out on the gossip and two was the sight of the woman who placed her hand into her father's. Even at this slight distance, he could see her perfection. Glossy brown hair, big, beautiful eyes and a curvaceous figure. He heard Anthony whistle under his breath, Lucas swore an oath and Jeremy stood there with his jaw dropped.

Charlotte, herself, was caught in a daze. There was a ballroom full of people staring at her. Some in awe, some with compassion and some with plain curiosity. Some of the men she saw watched her with a lascivious gleam in their eyes. In some of the women, she saw envy and there were some who stared at her with outright animosity! Hoping to make friends with similar ideals to hers, she kept her eyes peeled for a friendly face. She intended to embrace the stigma of a bluestocking and surround herself with like-minded ladies. Keeping her head held high, she continued with introductions on the arm of her father.

They came upon a guest who looked at her with tear-filled eyes. Concerned, she reached for her hand. Kentwell, who looked uncomfortable, introduced the Duchess of

Portsmouth, explaining she had been a friend of her mother's. Charlotte vaguely recalled the duchess from childhood visits, memories of her mother sipping tea and laughing with her friend.

"You are a vision of your mother, my dear. She would be so proud of you. She would always say how she could not wait to watch you take your place in society and she surely is watching over you now," the duchess said, squeezing her hand. *How kind*, she thought, genuinely touched by these heartfelt words, and squeezed her hand back.

"Thank you, your grace. I always love to hear about my mother. I hope we see each other over the season to talk more," she said with sincerity.

"Of course, we will, my dear. We will make arrangements. I really want you to meet my son Adam. You may have been too young to remember him. He is six years your senior. I wonder where he is."

The duchess looked around the room but could not see him. Smiling and nodding, Charlotte let out an unladylike snort in her mind as she put two and two together. She may not be out in the ton, but even she knew of the duchess's son, the notorious rake, Adam Langdon, the Marquess of Sunderland, and she had no desire to make his acquaintance. More memories slowly trickled back to her. She remembered meeting Adam, blonde and tall. She would have been six or seven and they had argued over something. Fish bait she thought, and he told her she was only a little girl and should be embroidering not fishing. I am no more a lady now than I was then, so an introduction was futile. And if rumours were true, he liked nothing more than a silly, gullible female. Something she certainly was not.

Adam, having shaken himself out of his trance, laughed softly to himself. He had seen many beautiful women and bedded just as many. *Perhaps I was just taken by surprise due to all the speculation*, he told himself. Charlotte's beauty and brains were a combination he had no desire to tangle with, not to mention her virginal innocence. Being leg shackled to such a chit would be exhausting. Seeing Kentwell taking her on the rounds, he realised he better escape before his parents called him over for an introduction. He bid Adele goodnight, extracted his arm and ignored her look of outrage. He informed his friends he would meet them for a night cap if they were not around by the time he returned and made his way over to Lady Isabel. Looking around carefully for a moment, he leaned down towards her and whispered in her ear to follow him out to the gardens. He exited inauspiciously, as only one with his rakish experience could, leaving Isabel a path to follow. He saw that Isabel, no stranger to a garden tryst, followed him with ease and he grinned at his luck.

Charlotte, feeling very flustered after so many introductions, told her father she needed to step out for fresh air for a few minutes. Dissuading any accompaniment, she wanted a few minutes in solitude. Luckily a waltz started and, as she could not yet dance, having not been officially presented at court, she was able to duck out unnoticed as the throng of people moved to dance.

Chapter Two

Unaccustomed to the ton, Charlotte was unaware that her departure was in fact seen. She was a new spectacle and there were two people who could not take their eyes off her. The Lady Adele was incensed with Adam's treatment of her and deeply jealous of the admiration she saw in his eyes when he gazed at Charlotte. The second, a gentleman the Viscount James Sheffield was also incensed but with lust, Charlotte's beauty, and wealth, he needed to have it. He resolved to make himself a permanent fixture at her side this season.

Chapter Three

Charlotte headed to the garden seat that had become her favourite spot: a bench that overlooked the roses. She sat down to breathe in the cool night air and inhale the fragrant tuberose. She was not too far, but far enough for the music to be faint, and was glad she had secured a private moment away from the swarm of guests. After a few seconds, she realised that there was a moaning sound coming from the nearby hedge and, with trepidation, she approached, instinctively knowing these moans were of a sexual nature. She peeked between the hedges and saw a man seated on a bench, his long legs on either side and his side profile facing her. Even in the moonlight, she saw he was a very handsome man. He wore his golden hair short and had a straight, aquiline nose and a strong, chiselled jawline. His eyes were closed, and a fair-haired woman sat astride him, their bodies moving against one another.

Realising that, again, she was engaging in voyeuristic behaviour, she turned to leave but her sleeve caught on a branch poking out of the hedge causing her to gasp out loud. She thought it was quiet enough that they would not have heard. *Surely the woman's loud moaning would mask it.* However, the woman stopped moaning.

"Langdon, why did you stop? I was almost ready to climax."

Groaning inwardly, she thought, *of course, the man debauching my garden is that rake Langdon.* She heard him shush the woman and send her off.

"I will make it up to you another time, but I worry we have been gone too long. Go inside and I will follow shortly." His voice was smooth and seductive, only enhancing her annoyance.

Charlotte heard the lady huff and swish away as her skirts rustled. Nervously, she hoped he would leave and not be curious to inspect the noise. Charlotte heard his footsteps and then they stopped. She felt a tingling sensation on her neck and, all of a sudden, knew she had to turn her head but she was filled with anxiety to do so. Taking a steady breath, she turned and came face to face with the most beautiful emerald-green eyes she could have ever imagined. Except they looked at her with distaste.

A sneer to match that look came upon his face.

"So, you are beautiful, smart and nosey – what a terrible combination, Lady Charlotte, an outright shrew."

Charlotte's mind was blank for a few seconds. *How can one so beautiful be so rude? He was not even ashamed about what she saw!* Remembering who she was and where they were, she drew herself up, despite being still attached to the hedge.

"I beg your pardon but you, sir, are in my garden, dallying like a most despicable profligate, while I have come out into my own garden for fresh air. And you accuse me as the wrongdoer. Shame on you! I demand you help me with my entanglement and leave me to go back inside, you cur!"

She used the haughtiest tone she could muster, seeing she was still attached to a hedge.

Adam shook his head, "a cur, am I?" He mumbled to himself that this lady had a lot to learn. *Still*, he thought, *her fiery outburst was extraordinarily passionate – and unexpected. No shrinking violet was this violet-eyed beauty*, he thought, laughing at his wit.

"I will help you, for I am a gentleman, most of the time," he said, giving her one of his wicked grins, "but I would pass advice that you do sound like a horrible shrew, which is not a desirable trait for a wife. Since I assume that is your plan this season, to land a husband."

Though even as he called her a shrew, he could not deny how breathtaking she was in her anger, nor could she deny that his arrogant manner was intriguing. Chemistry crackled in the air as he drew closer. The tension alarming them both as he untangled her sleeve and placed his arms on her shoulders. An actual spark of attraction jolted between them, and their eyes caught in surprise. To his own experienced passions, he knew this was something powerful and he could not compare it to anything he had ever felt. He could not help himself as he slowly descended his head to her upturned face, inhaling a pleasant scent of roses. Her pink pouty lips slightly parted in surprise and her eyes turned deep purple, starting to shutter close as he ever so gently pressed his lips to hers. Adam could tell this was her first kiss, the way she stood there like a statue, but he could sense she wanted more and the feeling that he was the first to kiss her caused a surge of primitive possessiveness to course through him. Increasing the pressure, he ran his tongue across the seam of his lips to soften and encourage her to open her mouth. He gained entry as she let out a slight, breathy moan and he touched his tongue to hers. The impact of this kiss was unprecedented, and he pulled her closer. She was also taken back. There was a tingling feeling that radiated heat throughout her body and she had the urge to press her body against his as all coherent thoughts flew out of her now senseless mind.

Before they could continue to explore each other's mouths, they heard footsteps approaching. Adam broke away and pulled Charlotte to the opposite side of the hedges. They stood still, Charlotte barely breathing, until they heard the footsteps walk away. Before Adam could turn to Charlotte fully, he felt little fists pounding his shoulder as he turned around and she began to berate him.

"My debut and set upon by the most notorious rake in the ton and almost ruined in my own garden. Do not think for one moment I am a prim and proper Lady that will not call you out."

Adam stared at her stunned, as he gripped her tiny hands and suddenly burst out laughing.

"Doth thinks my lady protests too much," he said, his laughter turning into a rakish grin showing his perfect, white teeth. She retorted snappishly.

"I am surprised you can even quote Shakespeare. Where did you find the time between drinking and fornicating?"

He lent down and whispered in her ear, "Are you angry at me or angry because of how much you enjoyed my kiss?" Before she could respond, he walked away, his stride arrogant and sure.

Charlotte faltered, only for a moment, before she digested his salacious words. *Protesting too much? Enjoyed his kiss?* She spun away in a whirl of fury. Picking up her skirts and throwing his retreating figure one last glare, she headed off back through the garden and into the ballroom.

Upon entering the ballroom, she made a beeline for her father, intending to stay by his side and well out of mischief for the rest of the night.

Adam returned to the ballroom and made his way to his friends. Lucas gave him a quizzical look that soon became laughter.

"How is it, old boy, that you left to dally with an eager lady who has returned looking quite dissatisfied, but you have come back looking quite satisfied? Usually, you are not such a selfish lover."

Lucas's words reminded Adam that his tryst did not turn out as expected, as he had forgotten all about Isabel. He turned to him and laughed.

"Yes, our tryst was cut short, neither was left satisfied, but I had a most pleasant and unexpected encounter. That is all I will share."

From the corner of his eye, Adam saw someone gesturing to him, and he turned to find his mother hailing him over. He excused himself from his friends for the second time that evening and, when he reached his mother, he saw that standing nearby was Charlotte and Kentwell. Charlotte's face was a mask of cool indifference and Adam thought, for such an innocent, she was fully adept at showing zero emotion, considering what they had just exchanged. He would have liked a little blush or any sign that she was affected.

"Adam, my dear son. Let me introduce you to Lady Charlotte, the daughter of the Duke of Kentwell, and Lady Charlotte please meet my son, Adam Langdon, the

Marquess of Sunderland and heir to the Duke of Portsmouth. You met in your youth you may recall." Lady Lydia beamed with the introduction and looked expectantly at them both. Charlotte lowered prettily into a curtsey and Adam bent forward with an elegant bow, captured her hand and kissed it with a "My Lady Charlotte, it is a pleasure".

Charlotte felt for sure someone would notice the impact this had on her. The combination of the warm touch of his mouth searing her hand and the deep timbre of his voice made her hand slightly tremble. Thankfully, as she gazed around, no one seemed to notice, except of course for Adam and, by God, did she want to smack that arrogant smirk from his face. *Infuriating rogue!* Adam, satisfied with her reaction, excused himself. Charlotte spied three young women around her own age standing near the far wall and she turned to her father, the Duchess and the few others in their circle and made her own excuses. She had seen them earlier and they had intrigued her. They were not fluttering around like the other women her age, looking to see if anyone was watching them. Instead, they were focused on their own conversation, their smiles and laughter genuine.

Charlotte made her way over and saw they were indeed young, seemingly close to her own age. They stared at Charlotte, a little in surprise, when she approached and requested introductions. The petite, curly haired blonde stated she was Lady Emma Finley, the tall, black-haired woman was Lady Harriet Howard and the curvaceous redhead Miss Eleanor Gibson. Charlotte could see these were no giggly debutantes, as each woman held an air of intelligence and shrewdness. Lady Emma broke the silence with a blunt comment.

"My Lady, I am not sure if you are aware of who we are, but we are the Wallflowers of last season. We know you are new to society, and we would not want to lead you astray. There is little we can do for your social standing."

Eleanor nudged Emma to hush her. Charlotte, in turn, laughed and provided an explanation to their befuddled expressions at her amusement to this statement.

"The Wallflowers, yes, I think I have found my group of friends; however, I believe what we are is intelligent women who will have lots in common. I prefer we call ourselves Bluestockings," as she smiled warmly at them in turn.

"And please let's not be Lady this and Miss that, let's simply be friends."

The three women looked at each other and with silent confirmation turned to her with welcoming warm smiles. She felt a weight lift from her shoulders. She had friends.

"Now, tell me, my friends. What have I missed out on all this time out of high society?" Emma linked her arm with Charlotte's, winking conspiratorially with the others, "We will need more then this moment. Let us plan our first intimate social event."

Adam was back amongst his friends, discussing a farming technique he was trialling at one of his estates with Anthony, when he overheard Jeremy ask Lucas a question.

"Lucas, pray tell. What are you staring at so intently?" The three gentlemen followed his line of sight and Anthony began to laugh, "That's going to be trouble." Jeremy added,

"That group of bluestockings adding that little gem to their ranks, god save us from intelligent lasses." His friends did not deny these ladies were lovely indeed, but he knew their perceptive expressions were more than rakes, as they, could take. Adam remained silent, while his friends joked, watching Charlotte's animated face as she conversed with her new friends.

Lucas who must have turned to watch him quietly said, "You have a most enamoured look on your face, my friend. Don't tell me one of the ton's most sought-after bachelors is about to be reformed?"

Adam, feeling foolish for being so obvious, denied the accusation. He felt, for his own self-preservation, that it was time to leave and suggested so to his comrades. Jeremy himself intended to visit Birds of Paradise, which was considered the most esteemed of brothels. Adam advised he would come along. He needed to ease the sexual frustration he was feeling. He ignored the part that was telling himself it was not coitus interruptus with Lady Pembroke that had left him inflamed but that scorching kiss he shared with Charlotte. He spared her one last glance before ignoring all good manners by not bidding farewell to the hosts or his parents and made a swift exit of Kent House.

Charlotte saw Adam make this quick exit and the glance he gave her; from a distance she could not make out his exact expression. Harriet noticed her focus and thought, as her new friend, it would be her place to impart some advice. Harriet had minimal experience with men herself, never being courted but had heard all the rumours just the same.

"Adam Langdon may be one of the most handsome in the ton but he appears to have no intentions to marry, his dalliances, plenty and many, are in this same ballroom. He never even spares a glance at the innocents," she said, pausing. Then she continued, "but he spared one for you."

Blushing and embarrassed about being caught out, Charlotte turned to Harriet.

"The Marquess is an old family friend, nothing more. Rest assured, despite my absence from society, I still managed to hear of all his scandalous exploits."

Harriet accepted this answer with a nod and the ladies continued to discuss plans for the season's balls, luncheons and dinner parties and activities of their own like teas and book discussions. They were eager to partake with Charlotte all the things they had taken for granted. Charlotte learned unique details about each of her new friends. Emma was a champion for causes. Eleanor was a talented singer and Harriet skilled with the pianoforte, both promising to assist Charlotte with her own lacklustre skills.

She continued to meet members of the peerage and several young men made her acquaintance as the night wore on but, as pleasant as they were, they caused no flicker of excitement the way that Adam had. Her only other memorable encounter was Viscount Sheffield, who genuinely seemed interested in her wit not her charms or fortune. He was tall and had brown hair and brown eyes, not handsome like Adam but still attractive. The ball came to an end sometime after midnight. Exhausted, physically and mentally, she fell into a deep sleep and, as soon as she laid her head upon her pillow, her last thoughts were of her very first kiss.

Adam awoke sometime around noon the following day with a throbbing headache and parched throat. Sitting on the edge of his bed, face in hands, he called for his valet Freddy to bring him coffee and water and to prepare a bath. As he went through his ablutions, his mind whirled with recollections of the previous night: Charlotte's kiss, the copious amount of whiskey and the courtesan or was it courtesans? The memory was just a mash up of flesh, but he somehow recalled being unable to take any pleasure.

"Christ," he said aloud and Freddy jumped up with, "Yes, milord?" Shaking his head in an attempt to rid himself of his thoughts, he told Freddy to have the stable hand saddle Argo, his horse, so he could head to his parents. He had planned to go over the estate books – hangover or not.

His bachelor townhouse in the middle of town, while ideal for his social life, was not where he liked to work. The office at Portsmouth House was his favourite room. His mind turned to the comforts of strong oak furniture, wood smoke from the fireplace and fine brandy and his mood was suddenly uplifted. As he rode to Portsmouth, he felt a trickling of guilt and attributed it to Charlotte. Shrugging, he thought, *who cares how I spent my evening? I am a bachelor.* Kissing an innocent was nothing to stress about and he would more than likely not bump into her throughout the season, seeing the different company they would keep. *Yes,* he told himself. It was absolutely nothing to concern himself with. But a niggling thought persisted. No woman had ever turned him inside out the way Charlotte had when he had kissed her.

Chapter Four

Adam handed Argo's reins to the stable hand, giving his brown fur a vigorous rub, and went in to greet his parents. He did not locate his mother and was advised his father was in the office. Adam found his father there, standing up and staring out the window.

"Good afternoon, Father. How do you fair today?"

"Well, my boy, well. I looked over the figures, and the investment you made in purchasing that new farm equipment has already enhanced our profits. You have a fine eye for business son. You always have."

"Thank you. It has made harvesting easier for our tenants as well."

Pleased with his father's compliment, he took a seat at the mahogany desk and began to work. He enjoyed the companionable silence until the door swung open without a knock.

He looked up to see his mother approaching with a steely eyed look of determination.

"Wonderful evening last night, was it not? To see the Lady Charlotte come out. She will be presented at court this week in time for the season to start."

She came and stood in front of Adam, and he looked up, fighting an urge to roll his eyes.

"Did you have any memories of her Adam?" she asked, looking at him intently.

"I recalled meeting her as children, yes. We bickered over fish bait. I daresay she is still a shrew," he said, laughing to himself at his little joke. His mother poked and probed him further and he was starting to become suspicious about where this was leading.

"I plan to spend time with her this season. She is dear to me like a daughter, you understand. Her mother was the dearest friend I ever had. And Kentwell was cordial, which I will accept as his way of letting bygones be bygones."

"That is wonderful mother. I am glad you are getting this opportunity."

"She is going to be sought after this season." Adam nodded but stayed silent.

Undeterred, she pressed on. "Such a fine, young woman she grew up to be: intelligent, beautiful and an heiress. It is my wish Adam that you court the Lady Charlotte this season and ask for her hand."

Father and son stared at the duchess, who suddenly appeared as immovable as a mountain, hands on hips ready to fight any dissention.

Adam could not help but find his mother's stance quite amusing. She was a diminutive, sweet-looking woman with the same thick, golden-blonde hair and emerald-green eyes he had inherited. He and his father both knew her looks were deceiving, as she was a force to be reckoned with once she put her mind to something. Adam, rather than become defensive, tried the flippant approach.

"Come now, Mother. Every season, you ask me to settle

down, but I am still not ready. Lady Charlotte is beautiful and smart but, alas, I do not need an heiress. Some charming but poor lord will snap her up."

He turned his attention back to his ledgers. Even as he said the words, he felt an unfamiliar sensation: jealousy, he surmised, at the thought of another man taking her innocence.

His mother broke into his thoughts with the most unexpected statement: "I saw you kiss her, Adam."

He heard his father's sharp intake of breath as Adam felt his own head bounce up, while his jaw dropped. She pressed on, somewhat dryly, no remorse in her tone.

"It is a known fact you make every effort to steer away from the innocent, unwed ladies and instead spend your time dallying with any other married woman, widower or strumpet that throws themselves at you."

Satisfied with her son's expression, she waved her husband off, as he asked why she had not told him. She gave him an imperious look.

"I did not tell anyone. I will not risk any scandal. And you, dear husband, may have forewarned our son of my plans." She turned back to Adam. "I think you felt something for Lady Charlotte and you, the Marquess of Sunderland, will be a man and pursue this." With one last steely glance at Adam, she spun on her heels and left.

Adam turned to his father, who wore a look of similar resignation.

The duke raised his hands, "Do not look to me in this. I will not challenge your mother and damnation. You know better than to go around kissing innocent ladies, son."

Scowling, he replied, "If she had come snooping a few minutes earlier, she would have caught me under the skirts of Pembroke's wife."

He gave Adam an admonishing look and stood up advising he would leave him to think about what his mother had demanded. For the second time that day, Adam held his head in his hands and suppressed a moan. He, the future Duke of Portsmouth, had just been ordered by his mother to leg shackle himself and the worst part was he actually felt a little twinge of excitement.

Charlotte had been busy. Adam had only popped into her thoughts every time she had found a moment alone. She had been presented at court and had had her new friends over for tea. She loved her witty new friends. *Today, I will be attending establishments rather than receiving visitors!* She was giddy with excitement at being swept away in the hustle of London. She planned to go to the modiste, the bookstore, the milliners, the haberdasher and to stop off at Gunter's for a lemon ice. Moving to the week ahead, she thought of what a whirlwind it would be. She had already secured her voucher to Almack's, the epitome of social standing. Well, her father had; it appeared everyone wanted to accommodate him. She knew her father was a powerful and influential man but was still surprised with all he had managed.

This reminded her of the viperous comments she had heard from the other ladies at court. More specifically, Ladies Eliza and Portia had both been sniping at how unfair it was that the 'spoiled duke's daughter' was receiving special treatment. She overheard them saying how unfortunate that the rumours were not true and if only she were hideous or hunchbacked. She asked her new friends if this was the talk circling about her and they had filled her in on the shallow gossip. They had also mentioned that there had been a betting book circling the men's clubs. Rather than be insulted, she found this hilarious since, on all accounts, they were all wrong! Her only hope was that Adam had not partaken. Shaking her head, she censured herself for allowing self-doubt to make her care what anyone thought.

Charlotte surmised Eliza was bitter after not making a match in her first two seasons. From what she heard, Portia was considered a diamond of the first water upon her coming out, but her mother had fallen ill and her season was cut short so she could return home. She felt she had been wronged. It was also rumoured Portia had her eye on one of the rich, titled, handsome lords, like Adam and his friends, and she intended for one to court her this season. She was not taking any competition lightly. Thinking of Adam's kiss, she wondered what he would do if he found himself alone with one of them. *Would he kiss them as well?* Scowling at the thought, she headed downstairs to meet Aunt Anne.

The day passed in a blur. Everywhere they went it seemed people wanted to lay praise and ask who had caught her eye for the season. She thanked those for compliments and laughed any questions off with a "time will tell" and a wink. Some of the older matrons gaped at her in surprise, and Aunt Anne's voice was persistent in her ear: *"Ladies do not wink"*. She was unfazed. They ordered an astonishing number of gowns and dresses for every occasion, as well as undergarments and redingotes. They then moved on to another list including accessories, reticules, parasols, and shoes. *Those two impertinent ladies may be right after all,* she thought wryly. *I am spoilt.* Though her two favourite purchases were her new books. The clothing item she was most excited for was a riding habit she designed herself, since the ones currently in fashion were just impractical in her view. Aunt Anne had cautioned her it was quite risky, but she did not care.

At Gunter's, Aunt Anne sipped her tea and Charlotte ate her lemon ice, savouring the tangy freshness, as she fingered the pages of her new books, Shakespeare's *Taming of the Shrew* (*ironic*, she mused since Adam had called her a shrew) and Mary Shelley's *Frankenstein or the Modern Prometheus*. She loved the smell of the printed paper and inhaled and exhaled contentedly, while her aunt looked on disapprovingly. She was eager to curl up and read the rest of the evening away. She hoped they were an entertaining read, as the memory of Adam had lurked in the back of her mind all day and she desperately needed a distraction.

Arriving home, the footman handed her a note from the Duchess of Portsmouth, and she thought wryly, *Instead of a distraction I get an invite from Adam's mother.* The duchess had spared no time in inviting her over for tea. Knowing she would not pry as much information from her father, she asked Aunt Anne to assist her in getting ready the following day, so she could ply her with questions.

Charlotte reflected on the response she had received from her aunt as she made her way over to meet the duchess. According to Aunt Anne, after her mother had passed, the duchess had told her father she would help raise her. She wanted Charlotte to spend part of the year with her as she got older so she could guide her in becoming a lady. Her father, mad with grief, was very angry in his rejection of her proposal and said she had no business suggesting such a thing. Aunt Anne believed that her father had grown to regret his harsh words, but both Charlotte and her aunt knew how stubborn he was. In retrospect, Charlotte was not mad at her father for denying her an opportunity, as she wanted for naught and there was no use in regrets. But she was very glad to now have the chance to be reacquainted with her.

"Why are you so excited, my love?" the Duke of Portsmouth enquired quizzically of his humming wife.

"Why dear husband, I have invited Lady Charlotte over," she said with a smile.

He laughed as realisation dawned on him.

"You are plotting and matchmaking!"

Nodding, she said, "Of course I am. I will not leave something like this up to chance and, by chance, I mean our son following good sense."

Blowing him a kiss, she headed to the garden to await Charlotte's arrival.

The Portsmouth townhouse was magnificent. It was as grand as Kent House, but there was an opulence Charlotte's own house lacked. *A woman's touch*, she mused, taking in the grandiose of the furniture and decor as she was led outdoors to the garden. The sun was peeking through the clouds lending warmth, and the landscaped foliage had a tropical feel she found very relaxing.

"Dearest, how glad I am you have arrived. Sit down, sit down," the duchess said, giving her a warm hug. Sitting down, she took a long look at her host and realised how much Adam looked like her, with the golden hair and emerald eyes.

The duchess was a superb conversationalist, and an hour flew by where she shared so much of herself easily. She noted that, every time Charlotte touched on a topic that may have led to awkwardness over the argument with her father, the duchess adeptly steered away. Not wanting any awkwardness, she decided to use her directness.

"Duchess, forgive me, but I just want to tell you that I know you and my father quarrelled. I have no ill will. You were both looking out for my best intentions." Her warm tone smoothed over the direct approach, or so she thought.

Laughing away the tears that had sprung into her eyes, the duchess said, "How like your mother you are with that direct tongue, and how I miss her. I am so happy that we have the opportunity to get to know one another."

Charlotte checked her own emotions, nodded and raised a new topic.

"I am going to Almack's tomorrow night. Will you be attending?" The duchess nodded.

"I will be in attendance. I count the patronesses as some of my dearest friends."

Before she could respond, the duchess said, "I will ensure Adam attends. I would love to see you two dance."

Blushing, she nodded. How could she respond to such a statement? The duchess used her silence to tell her about

Adam, and she could not help but feel intrigued as she learned more about him, his intelligence, his warm heart towards his tenants. There was more to him then his handsome facade and, despite knowing his rakish reputation, she could not help but want to know him better.

Chaperoned by Aunt Anne and her father, Charlotte attended Almack's and it was here that she saw the ton in its element. The crowd appeared more comfortable in their talk and laughter, more so than court, and were openly staring at her. She heard whispers about her unladylike mannerisms: *"Her gait is strong like a man"*; how much her dowry was worth: *"If you beget a few sons on her, you pass on your own title and get her father's title for another"*; and other bits of idle gossip. *So,* she thought with a frown, *this is what these petty people think.* Clearly their silly bets did not suffice. Her father must have noticed her expression, as she felt him pat her shoulder.

"Pay them no mind, my dear. You will soon see certain ton gatherings are akin to stepping on a hornet's nest, lots of buzzing and chatter and none too kind. You just remember who you are. You are a Fitzroy of Kentwell, and you hold your head high."

Charlotte gave her father a peck on the cheek and straightened her spine. Aunt Anne drew her attention next.

"Is that not your new friends over there by the far wall?"

Following her Aunt's gaze, she nodded. Her father and Aunt had taken to her friends, unsurprised she had befriended likeminded ladies, though she admitted her friends were still much more refined than herself.

"Yes, it is. May I go say hello and spend some time with them?" she asked, turning to her father.

"Of course. While you do that, I am going to play a round of cards," he said, with a parting pat on her back. Her father headed off and Aunt Anne rolled her eyes.

"I will escort you over and go find some ladies I would like to be reacquainted with."

Chapter Five

Adam tried to refrain from looking for Charlotte after the earful he had copped from his mother. Not only had she forced him into attending Almack's – a social setting he disliked – but she was also insisting he ask her to dance. His mother knew very well that he avoided things like dancing when possible. Dancing with impressionable chits out on a season caused rumours and unwanted attachments. Despite his efforts to pay her no attention, he could not help but stare when he caught glimpses of her beauty, made easy with the brightly lit chandeliers suspended from the ceiling.

He was with his friends and some other gents and had spied her frowning. Kentwell said something that brought a smile to her face and made her stand tall. Her confidence, he found, was very attractive. Shaking his head and cursing himself, he turned his back to the conversation. Lord Percy had just finished asking who was intent on courting Charlotte and who would have the most luck.

"They will have to get past Kentwell's scrutiny first," laughed Lucas.

"I hear she is quite a hoyden. I daresay whoever holds

her interest will have his hands full," Lord Percy said, waggling his eyebrows. "And I mean that figuratively and physically." Adam threw him a scowl, but Lord Percy's head was turned. Anthony, however, caught it and gave him a confused look.

Adam glanced at her again, soaking up the vision she made in a midnight blue gown with a silver diaphanous material layered over the top. The intensity of the colour accentuated her creamy skin, and her vibrant brown tresses were swept up in a flattering up do that showed off the elegant slope of her neck. *Where did that come from?* he asked himself with a start. *Now I am spouting off like a besotted fool.* Disgusted with himself, he tried to pay attention to the conversation. Another gentleman, Viscount James Sheffield, had joined in the laughter and was speaking.

"Well, I have just espied Kentwell heading off so I will be using this time to my advantage."

With a smug look at the rest of them, he farewelled the group. Lucas who was standing next to Adam questioned in a low tone, "What is the matter? You look vexed."

Adam was taken aback that his thoughts were again on show so transparently. He shrugged it off as nothing but saw Lucas still eyeing him curiously. To his other side, he heard Anthony grumble in objection.

"Those two blonde chits are staring over here again giggling and seeking our attention," Anthony informed his friends.

"I am in the mood for dancing, so I am happy to oblige one, but I need a second, gents. Who is coming with me?" Jeremy asked his friends.

Anthony's only answer was another objection and

Adam simply grunted so Lucas, with a resigned sigh, agreed.

"Come on, let us dance, but no walks in the garden. Those two are just looking to be compromised."

Charlotte accepted a dance from Viscount Sheffield, informing him he would have to wait as she promised the next quadrille to another. As that dance started, her partner, some Lord of something she had no interest in, was wearing on her nerves. He held her too close during the waltz and his breath smelt stale as he droned on pompously.

"You dance quite well, my dear, for someone who has lived in seclusion. You just need to work on refinement," he advised her, smiling as if he expected her to thank him.

"My Lord, I was not in seclusion. I had a full and rich upbringing and I do not base my accomplishments around dance," she said loudly, with her eyes narrowed.

"I can see your manners need some refining as well. You should not correct your betters, and in such a tone as well," he said reprovingly.

She gritted her teeth to hold back a retort. They danced past others and she caught the eye of the Earl of Chester, who smiled at her in sympathy, while his dance partner Portia gave her a smug stare. Angry that she had been reprimanded by this prig and someone had heard, she decided decorum was not worth her dignity.

"You, sir, are not my better. I am the daughter and heir to an esteemed duke. I do not even recall your title, it was so insignificant." For added impact, she brought her foot down hard on his. He yelped in pain and shock and looked at her aghast. She gave him one final contemptuous look and stalked away with her head held high.

She heard the Earl of Chester's bark of laughter and Portia gasp, but she cared naught for anyone's opinion.

Charlotte returned in a fury to her friends. They had observed her lack of grace but, of course, instead of being scandalised, they rallied around her. She told them what he had said as she watched some of the other guests point at her, as their mouths moved wildly.

"My impetuousness is really not a good combination mixed with the ton," she mumbled to her friends, "but there is only so much I can take."

"Do not fret. Gossip passes, and you are the daughter of a Duke. All they can do is gossip," said Emma, pragmatic as always.

Adam had been watching her dance and could see how tense her posture was and how frustrated her expression was. He was unsurprised when he saw her stamp her foot on the pompous fool she was dancing with. Chuckling, he marvelled at her boldness. Lucas returned, and Adam asked what had happened.

"He insulted her lack of refinement and referred to himself as her better. Lady Charlotte was having none of that and gave him a verbal uppercut and stomped on his foot," Lucas told him, tears of mirth in his eyes.

"By God, Langdon, it was good to see a lady act with some spirit. I think this little group of bluestockings may be the bright spark of what was to be another dull season."

Adam nodded in agreement. He could not help but be

intrigued by Charlotte he decided, even if it was not easy to admit. More flashbacks came to him as he remembered the precocious child she had been and how she had enjoyed challenging anything he said. *It is funny*, he wondered. *I have only met her a handful of times as children, but she still made an impression.*

Laughing still at her antics, he turned to his friend, but he could not help but sneak another look at her soon after. He saw Sheffield was now by her side. The music for a quadrille started up and Sheffield offered Charlotte his hand to escort her to the floor. Adam was disturbed to realise that an angry, possessive feeling was coursing through his veins. Jealousy, again! Searching for distraction, he caught the eye of Lady Grace, a past affair, her revenge on a cheating husband, and saw her giving him a seductive look. Anthony saw the look and asked if Adam wanted to attend to some personal business but, surprising them both, he shook his head. "You know what? I think I will have a dance."

Charlotte was annoyed with herself for she could not help her attention moving to Adam. Even at a distance, she saw him smiling and laughing, enhancing his good looks. She had an attentive, charming viscount treating her with respect and who clearly did not mind her 'mannish gait' or lack of 'refinement' but here she was keeping tabs on Adam to see if he was dancing with anyone. She allowed the viscount to lead her to the dance and saw people watching, probably wondering if she was going to step on his foot. As they finished their dance, he escorted her back to her friends and politely offered to obtain refreshment for everyone.

Watching him walk away, Harriet giggled.

"He is eager to impress. How will he carry four drinks back?"

"With Charlotte in tow this season, we will be waited on hand and foot," Eleanor joked.

"Unless she stomps on another foot," Emma quipped, making them all laugh.

"I am only living up to my hoyden status," she laughed, unperturbed, knowing her friends jested in goodwill.

Sheffield returned, two drinks in tow but with a friend carrying the other two, and the ladies all laughed and gave their thanks. Charlotte let herself relax, as she was enjoying the camaraderie with her friends. Emma suddenly nudged her with a sharp elbow.

"The Marquess is beelining straight for you."

Charlotte looked up and her heart began to beat faster in excitement as she saw the golden-haired man stalk towards her, reminding her of a majestic lion – not the king of the jungle but the king of the ton.

Adam realised there were several pairs of eyes on him as he crossed the room and headed for Charlotte, but he did not care. As soon as her eyes met his, he sensed her excitement, and it encouraged his own. Ignoring the warning look he was getting from Sheffield and trying not to smile in humour at her bluestockings friend, who stood around her in defence, he gave a small bow.

"May I have your hand in a dance, Lady Charlotte?"

She waited a few seconds before replying and he wondered for a wild moment whether she was going to say no. Her expression was unreadable and his heart pounded anxiously.

"Of course, thank you for asking. The dance about to start is free on my card." Exhaling, he gave her one of his most sensual smiles as he held out his hand, "May I?"

Charlotte and Adam felt the stares as they moved around the dancefloor in a lively waltz. She could not help but be impressed with Adam's dancing, his movements so sure and confident. He could feel the tension in her body but knew it was not because of him, but something else. The staring perhaps? He also could not help but notice how much he enjoyed touching her, even the simple caress of her small palm in his and his other hand cresting on her lower back. Clearing his throat, he bent closer to her, inhaling her intoxicating scent of roses, which did not aid his already befuddled senses.

"What is the matter? You seem very tense." He was surprised when he saw her blush slightly.

"If you must know, I do not feel very accomplished with dancing. This is new to me." He loved her forthrightness and, knowing she may be thinking of her previous dance, he smiled softly.

"You dance just fine. I surely have no complaints," he said in a reassuring tone.

Not wanting to let her know he and Lucas had been gossiping like old matrons, he did not bring it up. Surprised by his genuine support, she could not help but recall their meeting in the gardens and narrowed her eyes.

"You had a complaint last I saw you, or were you so imbibed you do not recall?"

Bemused, he responded in kind.

"You certainly are direct, my lady and I must say I like it. But yes, I do recall."

"If a lady cannot speak her mind and be on equal standing, maybe I do not want to be a lady," she said, her chin lifting stubbornly. She ignored the last remark as the blush heating her face was bad enough. Waiting for censure or taunts, she realised he stared at her with admiration instead and her heart clenched. *The rogue understands me. How odd out of all people,* she thought.

"I find we are very much on equal standing. I find myself having respect for you like no other lady I have met. You can always speak your mind to me."

"I will hold you to that, Langdon," she warned, but with a small smile, feeling shy all of a sudden.

"Did you take bets against me prior to my ball?" she asked, watching his face for any sign of lies.

"No. I found it immature. I also had the advantage of remembering you. You are just as I remember you as a child, strong and wilful, but I find it no longer annoys me like when I was a boy. I respect you are a lady who knows her own mind."

Her eyes widened as she absorbed his unexpected praise. He suddenly felt a need to run, as foreign emotions swelled within him. The music ended, signalling the end of the dance, and he bid her a hasty farewell, leaving her dumbfounded at their exchange.

Adam made his way over to his friends, who were staring at him strangely.

"Ah, Langdon," said Jeremy. "What the hell has gotten into you?"

He did not reply, as he did not know the answer. Charlotte was stirring emotions and feelings he had no experience with, and they made him nervous. *I need to keep my distance*, he told himself. My mother can take her matchmaking elsewhere.

"Come on, gents. Let us go find ourselves a card game," he said, changing the topic completely. Lucas, Jeremy and Anthony lifted their brows at one another but said nothing as they followed him. Lucas looked back at Charlotte and saw her eyes following Adam. Adam was so caught up in his own angst he had not even noticed.

Returning to her own friends, Charlotte knew she would have no answers for their questions. Sheffield, she noted, was no longer there. She looked around and saw him speaking with another lady who was giggling at him. Curiously, she realised it did not even give her a flicker of jealousy.

"Well, Charlotte, since when are you and the Marquess on such terms?" asked Emma.

"Tea with his mother, dancing at Almack's, is that wedding bells we hear in your future?" teased Eleanor.

She smiled at her friends and brushed their questions

off with a laugh. "As if I would ever take that rogue seriously."

Aunt Anne came over and whispered, "A lady does not stamp her foot on a gentleman's feet,"_though she said it with a devilish twinkle in her eye, knowing he had deserved it.

"I better go explain to your father, though I daresay he will find the whole thing highly amusing," she said, walking off with a grin on her face.

Charlotte steered the conversation to a suggestion Emma had made, that they make a book society club for likeminded young women to come together and discuss literature they would have to read on a monthly basis. She nodded along as she saw, from the corner of her eye, Adam taking his leave. The sinking pit in her stomach was a reminder that she could wave off disinterest to her friends but not to her own self, and she hoped to see him again soon.

"Milord, milord." Adam heard Freddy's voice through his tired and pounding head. Pulling himself awake, it dawned on him he had spent another night drinking, and he wrinkled his nose at the strong alcohol smell that clung to his clothes.

"What is it, Freddy?"

"Ah, milord, the duchess was here. I told her you were, uh, indisposed and she said to wake you, dress you and send you back to the family home so she could drum some sense into you." Freddy said the last words tentatively. "Her words, milord, not mine!"

Scowling, he got up and grumbled.

"Do not fret. I know very well what my mother is about."

As he bathed, he decided he would not go and see his mother. He sent one of the footmen with a note that he had to ride to one of the estates for a few days. Smiling, he thought this a great idea. He could escape the duchess's machinations and hopefully clear his mind of Charlotte.

"Come, Freddy. Get my bags packed and Argo saddled. We are going away for a few days."

Chapter Six

Charlotte had attended a few more events and began to understand how the ton worked. She remained a curiosity in the limelight regardless of what whispers circled about her behaviour. Her friends found it amusing that her popularity had also brought them out of the shadows, receiving more attention than usual. She had noted that the gentlemen, after a few turns around the ballroom, had realised this bunch of bluestockings weren't such a bore after all. It warmed her heart that her wonderful friends were getting the attention they had always deserved. She further observed the consternation of the other unwed ladies who usually enjoyed all these attentions. She had made no other close female friendships which suited her just fine. She did find though that the more men she spoke with the less impressed she was with her options. She grimaced at the memory of the interactions.

"What pursuits do you enjoy for your leisure, Lady Charlotte?" asked a bland-faced Earl during a dance.

"I enjoy riding and, back home on the estate, would

often race and jump hurdles with the stable boys," she offered. Horses were always a good topic.

"That must be very difficult to do side saddle," he had replied with an incredulous look. She had scoffed, knowing it was unladylike, and heard Aunt Anne's voice telling her, *"A lady does not scoff"*.

"I ride astride, of course."

"Now you are back amongst the civilised, my dear, side saddle it will be. I would not have a wife embarrass me so riding like a man throughout Hyde Park."

She was glad the dance had ended moments after his reply, as she had had to grit her teeth and refrain from a biting retort. She did not say as much as 'thank you' and just left him standing there, no doubt astounded by her lack of manners. He should think himself lucky he didn't get his foot stomped on, though she was coming to think the gossip had not taken after similar conversations with other lords. After everything from her opinions (*'A lady does not need to worry about what goes in Parliament'*) to playing billiards (*'That is not a game for ladies'*), she missed Adam. At least he was happy for her to speak her mind.

When shopping together, she had learned from the duchess that he was away on estate business. She did not delve further, mindful of the women they passed from store to store, having ears turned their way for gossip. The duchess had taken her under her wing, which was easily explained to all by the close friendship she had had with her mother. But Charlotte could not help but be suspicious that the duchess had an agenda to matchmake her with Adam. She kept bringing up various events of the social calendar. Countess Waltham was hosting her first dinner party, the Clifford's were holding a lavish ball as were the Stonewalls.

Being a practical person, she could not marry a man

that would no doubt carry on affair after affair, no matter how much he made her heart flutter or yearn to see him. The only potential suitor she did not mind was the Viscount James Sheffield. He was attractive, friendly and an avid reader, so they had much to discuss whenever he sought her out. True, he did not stir the passionate feelings she felt when within Adam's close proximity, but in hindsight Charlotte thought maybe that was not such a bad thing.

The next time she saw Adam was at a dinner party being hosted by a newlywed couple from last season, the Walthams. The sharp lyrical sounds of the strings of the cello and violin created an upbeat atmosphere that everyone was enjoying. It had been a week since she had last seen him at Almack's and she found herself eager for the sight of him. He truly was a beautiful specimen of a man. When their eyes met across the room, she was surprised that this time apart had not lessened the intensity of his presence and, upon eye contact, it seemed to draw a line straight between them. She felt a shiver go up and down her spine.

Viscount Sheffield appeared and drew her attention, and she tore her gaze away from Adam. He gave a deep bow and complimented them all on how lovely they looked. Charlotte beamed at her friends and wholly agreed. Harriet was in a lovely pale pink gown, which flattered her pale skin, dark hair, and luminous grey eyes. Emma was in a soft blue, which brought out the blue of her eyes and complimented her fair skin and strawberry blonde locks. Eleanor in sage green was striking, the colour setting off her red tresses and emphasising her eyes. She herself was wearing a deep purple tonight with her mother's amethyst and knew from the envious looks she received from the women and the appreciative looks from the men she made a pleasing image.

Her group turned when they heard high-pitched laughter that pierced their conversation. She saw Portia and Eliza speaking with Adam and his friends. Portia, it appeared, was trying every coquettish trick to keep Adam's attention, the downcast eyes and fluttering lashes, her fan beating against her bosom to draw his eye contact. Charlotte had sat in a few drawing rooms now where she had over-heard these little tricks. The silliest one she had heard was taking any opportunity to swoon where the gentleman would have to catch and hold her in his arms. Her scoffing in indifference made it no surprise to her as to why she made no new friends. Turning her back on the spectacle, she kicked herself that she had missed his company.

Adam was fighting the impulse to not stuff his cravat into Portia's mouth. This was a prime example as to why he did not deal with naive chits. To his own annoyance, he could not keep his gaze from flickering over to Charlotte. He truly thought this obsession would have passed. He had no urge to take a woman to bed; he had taken a bloody book instead! He saw Sheffield fawning over her, and rage swept over him. He wanted to remove his cravat again, this time to shove in Sheffield's mouth. She was not even wearing a fichu in her bodice and, even from this distance, her creamy cleavage was on display. He saw his friends throwing him confused glances and he caught Lucas's eyes. He nodded to

Portia, who was hanging off him, and shot Lucas a silent plea for rescue.

To his relief, Lucas fell upon his sword and turned his charm on Portia, who eagerly lapped it up. Reflecting, he thought that it was not as if Portia wasn't attractive. She was quite beautiful, but she lacked the genuine warmth that Charlotte had. *I need to sort out this obsession and have her once and for all.* Looking over again, he saw that Sheffield had his hand on her elbow and, like a man possessed, he stormed over.

"Excuse me, Sheffield. I must say hello to Lady Charlotte and secure a spot on her dance card."

Charlotte stared at him blankly as he turned his most dashing smile on her, his straight white teeth set off by his tanned face. He pressed an open-mouthed kiss on her hand.

"I have been out of town and not yet had the pleasure to dance with you. Please tell me you have a free spot?"

Reeling from the searing heat his kiss had left on her hand, she said a little breathlessly,

"Of course, my lord. I have quadrille and a waltz. Which would you prefer?" She damned this reaction he brought out in her.

As she chanted in her mind, *Please say quadrille*, the less intimate of the two, his grin turned devilish, "The waltz of course, my lady, and, if no one has claimed the right to escort you to dinner, please allow me to do the honours."

As luck would have it, no one had asked her that either. The Duchess of Portsmouth suddenly appeared with a mischievous twinkle in her eye.

"Just the two I was looking for. The countess has had to make some last-minute seating changes due to a few guests not arriving, so you two will be seated with each other." She hurried off before either could reply. Adam and Charlotte stared at each other at this obvious attempt to throw them together. Electricity crackled between them. Sheffield, not wanting to be forgotten and annoyed with Adam's interruption, cleared his throat.

"Charlotte, I know you have me down for a waltz already," he said, looking pointedly at Adam, "but, if it is all right with you, please put me down for the quadrille as well."

Adam's eyes narrowed dangerously at Sheffield, and Charlotte fought the urge to roll her eyes at this display of masculine power play.

"Of course," she replied and turned to Adam. "Mayhap, we should make our way to dinner, my lord?" She took his arm.

Not ignorant of her friends' amusement, she saw them holding back laughter as this strange exchange unravelled. Since when did Adam care who she danced with and want to dance with her himself? And he had called her a nosy shrew! He escorted her to dinner, their arms intertwined, and she blushed at the tension still building between them, wondering if he felt it too. Chancing a look, their eyes met, and she saw his eyes burning with the same intensity she could feel. Quickly looking away, she gulped nervously and thought, *This is going to be one very long evening indeed if I cannot control my reaction to this tempting rogue.*

Adam was struck with fascination at what Charlotte was bringing out in him while they sat in a busy dining room. He could see she was nervous and watched as she toyed with her chicken smothered in rich cream. He knew she was feeling the exact same way he did. However, every time he tried to engage her in conversation, he only received curt responses. Searching for another topic, he asked her what she had been reading. She laughed and he could not help but notice the radiance her smiling laughter brought to her face. She was beautiful, even with her aloofness, but she was breathtaking when she shone her light upon him. Her violet eyes mesmerised him, and he was itching to run his fingers through her rich brown tresses and to taste those pouty pink lips again.

"Do you remember when we met in the garden? You called me a shrew. Well, you inspired me to buy a copy of Taming of the Shrew and I do agree that Katherine and I have much in common, for I am headstrong and wilful too." Before he could reply, she continued, "Though I was displeased with the ending. I have now moved on to Shelley's Frankenstein."

Adam's own Adonis-like face lit up. Out of all the possible coincidences, he had not imagined this.

"I have been reading that as well! I have been at my estate, Hallend Manor, and the evenings get quite lonesome. I found a copy and, before I forget, please let me apologise for calling you a shrew. If truth be known," he lowered his voice, "I have not been able to stop thinking of you, making you more vixen than shrew."

Blushing furiously with his blatant flirting, she made to curtail her feelings and remembered she was no simpering miss.

"I would wager that was not the first or last time you used a similar line tonight, my lord," she said, her tone tart.

Hiding his disappointment at her obvious poor opinion of him, especially as he was being sincere, he flashed a smile. As luck permitted, they were both saved from an awkward moment when Jeremy, who was a few chairs down, asked Adam to weigh in on a debate he was having about curricles versus phaetons. During this reprieve, Charlotte took the time to study Adam. He was surely one of the tallest men she had ever seen and his shoulders were so very broad. She could not help but imagine what he would look like with his shirt off. Was he tanned all the way past his neck? Turning back to the table, she caught the end of a question the lord next to her was asking, "...demurer than rumours have foretold, Lady Charlotte."

"Pardon me, my lord?" Her voice was frosty at his implication.

"I simply make an observation, my dear. Rumour had it Kentwell had raised quite the hellion." He chuckled to himself. Feeling her ire raised, she took a deep breath.

"No. My father raised me to be of an equal standing with the opposite sex, not inferior," she replied, turning her back before he could respond.

Adam heard the exchange but refrained from intervening, understanding the importance she held on standing up for herself, but it did not make the urge to wipe that look of censure off the old fool's face any less. Before he could say anything to her, her first dance claimed her and, as she walked away to the dance floor, Adam got up to follow.

The strains of the music filtered through the ballroom as the orchestra played a lively tune signalling the dancing was about to begin. As she danced, she saw he was not dancing with anyone, just standing with his friends. She could feel him watching her, which caused a shiver of excitement to run down her spine. When it was time for the waltz with Sheffield, the intensity of Adam's gaze changed, and he did not even attempt to hide his displeasure. She noted, the viscount was dancing closer than usual, and she was not sure she liked it. Adam seethed with jealousy as he watched Sheffield's arms on her, his head leaning down to whisper in her ear, making her laugh.

Aunt Anne stood on the sidelines of the dancing with some ladies including Almack partonesses Countess Cowper and Viscountess Castlereagh. The group was content in watching the dancing unfold instead of joining in. It was not long before Charlotte danced past them on the arm of Sheffield.

"Your niece has caused quite a sensation already this season. She is incomparable; she looks so much like her mother," stated Countess Cowper.

"Yes, and I must say I have enjoyed hearing about her antics. It may not be societal expectations for a young lady to have such a spitfire personality, but I find it refreshing." The group chuckled. Aunt Anne also laughed but indulgently.

"Yes, my Charlotte is very fiery. It has always given me solace knowing she can take care of herself. Despite my reminders of how a lady behaves, I secretly get a thrill on how unorthodox she is! My brother raised her as he would a son, you see." Her friends all nodded at the explanation and, shortly after, caught sight of her again but with Adam. They soon lost them in the crowd.

"Ah, do not her and the Marquess of Sunderland make a beautiful couple?" sighed Viscountess Castlereagh.

"I hear the Duchess of Portsmouth is very keen on seeing that happen. It must be difficult having a son with proclivities of the flesh with no sign of settling down."

Anne listened to the ladies gossip and, while she knew he had a reputation, she also could see what the Duchess saw: that they would be perfect for each other.

"If anyone can tame that rogue, rest assured my Charlotte can."

Another Almack patroness, the Countess of Jersey joined the group and heard the last bit of their conversation.

"I heartedly agree. That is one match I would like to see."

By the time it was his turn to claim his waltz with Charlotte, his mood had not improved. As she took his hand and allowed him to lead her to the dancefloor, he had an idea, but the music was loud, making it hard to talk. Looking around, he saw the dance floor was quite full but there was enough space for him to manoeuvre her to the glass doors that led to the gardens. As the orchestra played the sheet music to the Sussex waltz, he looked Charlotte directly in the eye. He could see her watching him with a befuddled expression, and he found her quite adorable as her scent of roses tantalised his senses. He knew he should not be playing with fire and should just turn around and go back inside.

Chapter Seven

Adam as usual chose the reckless path, pulling her into darkness before anyone could notice. Charlotte started to raise protest, but he raised a glove covered finger to her lips. "Hush, I just wanted a moment alone with you." He had intended to talk but, having her alone for this brief period, he could not help himself. She did not protest as he stared deeply into her eyes, the emerald pools mesmerising. Neither did she resist when he lowered his lips to hers, touching her own gently. Glad she didn't pull away, he sucked on her lower lip, and she could not help the soft moan that escaped. That was all the encouragement he needed as he placed one hand to her lower back to pull her closer, using the other to tilt her head to kiss her deeply as their bodies pressed against each other. He placed his tongue in her mouth and felt her start then relax, as she tentatively touched his back with her own. He was firm and deft with his strokes, and she began to match his actions until his own groan vibrated through his chest against her own. He tore his lips away for much needed air but, instead of returning to her lips, his head lowered to her neck.

Charlotte felt him press wet, hot kisses against her neck and she sighed. *He is so hard and hot everywhere*, she thought in a daze. She had never dreamed these caresses could create such an inferno insider her body. She pressed into him even closer when he gently nipped at her earlobe. She rubbed herself against him and now he was the one who moaned. Charlotte heard the orchestra striking new chords and she suddenly broke away, but she did not get very far as he did not release her from their embrace.

He was shocked by the words that left his mouth, words he had never said, never wanted to say.

"Charlotte, give me a chance, get to know me, allow me to court you. I have not been able to stop thinking of you." His voice was low but insistent as his eyes searched her face for a reaction. The insanity of the situation she had just allowed herself to get caught up in washed over her. Was this a joke? Is this not the same man notorious for treating commitment like a plague? Staring into his eyes there was a possessive fire that frightened and excited her at the same time. She shook her head unable to form the words and removed his arm from her waist and rushed off. *This is madness*, she told herself. *Even if I want his suit how could it ever last?*

Frustrated that she had given him no answer, he cursed out loud. The shake of her head said no but her ardent response to his touch said yes. Not trusting himself to go back inside and face her, he skirted around the ballroom to the foyer, only to hear his mother calling out after him.

"You are leaving so soon? But what of Lady Charlotte?" Adam gave her a bitter laugh. "Well, mother, you have gotten your way. It appears I find myself enamoured with the Lady Charlotte." This time it was he who spun on his heel and walked away.

Lady Adele had followed the spectacle as the evening wore on, losing sight of them on the dancefloor. Frustrated and angry that Adam was acting lovesick over this silly chit, her thoughts turned spiteful. *If Langdon thinks he is going to get a happily ever after, he can think again.* She washed down her jealousy with a flute of champagne in one mouthful, as she bitterly surveyed the room.

Adam awoke the next morning in better spirits than usual. He had no hangover, no cloying scent of a woman's heavy perfume. In fact, to his satisfaction, the light scent of roses was still present. *Or is that just my mind playing tricks?* Thinking of how she felt in his arms and the raw passion she exuded caused him to grow hard. *Besotted fool I am, obsessed with a chit and a bluestocking to boot,* he thought shaking his head ruefully. Whatever the lingering scent was, it reminded him how stupid he was thinking he could win her over by just kissing her, that holding her in his thrall just for the moment would make her succumb to him. Charlotte was no over sexed woman who was intent on hunting him down to bed. "Maybe this is my karma," he pronounced out loud. It would not surprise him if it was, even he knew he had much to atone for with how he had spent his years. Still muttering, he got dressed, paying no heed to his valet who was standing nearby.

"Pardon, my lord?" asked Freddy.

"Nothing, just talking to myself like the fool I am. Carry on."

"Yes, my lord." Freddy shook his head. He had never seen the marquess befuddled before.

Adam was coming to understand his problem was that he had never had to woo a woman. His easy, roguish charm had always worked fine on its own. Women were always eager to fall into bed. And the intention here was to not get her into bed, not yet anyway, but try her hand at courtship. He realised he needed to make some genuine gestures and spend real time with Charlotte so she could see beyond his reputation and believe he had honest intentions. Adam now found it ludicrous that he was willing to settle in the future, marry someone dull to bore his heirs. Charlotte's beauty inflamed him, her intellect and wit enthralled him, and he knew without a doubt there would never be a boring moment by her side. He could not recall ever just enjoying conversing with a woman about books and exchanging banter.

He leaned back in the chair at his desk, hands entwined and tucked beneath his head. He grinned at the ceiling. Plans were starting to take shape in his mind and the thrill of the hunt began to hum through his veins. He imagined her shiny chestnut hair, unbound, his hands running through it, kissing, staring into her unique violet eyes and was eager to see her again. Let the official wooing of the Lady Charlotte begin.

"Freddy, have Argo saddled. We are going to visit the duchess."

When Charlotte awoke, she was tired from a restless sleep filled with tossing and turning. "Thanks to bloody Langdon," she grumbled to herself. She simply could not figure him out! Why had this notorious rake decided to play such wicked games with her? Everyone knew he was against marriage.

"Sorry, my lady? I did not catch that," Macy said.

"Oh, it was nothing, just grumbling to myself over the evening's event," she responded still deep in thought.

"Did a fine lord catch your eye?" Macy teased.

Charlotte's response was an unladylike grunt. Macy just chuckled. Charlotte knew she was obsessing, but what exactly did his behaviour mean? She finished her ablutions and walked downstairs to see what the day held, determined not to think of his handsome face. Her entrance to the drawing room halted all thoughts of Adam, just for a moment, as she took in today's flowers, which always followed an evening out. Despite her own feelings towards these pompous fools, they remained undeterred. "Due to my dowry," she grumbled to herself.

But a bouquet of roses caught her eye. They were not just any roses; they were a purple shade, a light lavender, so akin to her own eyes. *How wonderful*, she had never seen this shade before. Admiring their beauty, she moved towards them in wonderment and inhaled their sweet fragrance. She reached for the card and was pleasantly surprised when she read the words out loud:

Your scent is that of the sweetest rose, your loveliness surpasses any rose-filled garden and the roses I bestow on thee would still pale in the beauty of your eyes. Please allow me to take you for a picnic in the park tomorrow. Adam.

Usually, she found these sappy words cringeworthy, but not this time. She chuckled at his attempt at poetry but was flattered all the same. How does he know I love roses? Aunt Anne and Macy, who followed behind her, shared a bemused glance but one cross look from Charlotte sent Macy to prepare tea and Aunt Anne to start her embroidery. Falling back into a chair, a rose in hand that she tapped against her chin, she pondered the words of this man who is known for having dishonourable intentions. Bringing the rose close to her nose, she wondered where he had found these amazing roses. She could not help but be touched that he had gone to such efforts. However, her sense and sensibility did not allow her to fall apart as most ladies in her position would, so she remained wary and cautious while mulling over her reply. Feeling a mischievous grin grow on her face, she came up with the perfect response.

Adam was still in residence at his parents' home when Charlotte's note arrived. He was feeling pleased with himself, though he had to credit his mother who had requested her friend Lady Helen clip some of her prize, hybrid, purple roses. When he had told the duchess that he wanted to send Charlotte something unlike anything else she would be no doubt receive, he kept musing over her eyes. The duchess noted his fixation on how unique her eyes were, and the duchess knew then where they could obtain such a complimentary gift. Adam accepted the note from the footman and went to sit in his favourite armchair in the office with a snifter of brandy. With the confident assumption a rogue of his standing would have, he thought Charlotte had sent him back a 'yes'. His eyebrows lifted in surprise and lowered back down in amusement as he read her note.

My lord, these roses are by far the most beautiful I have seen, and your compliments do flatter me so. You may not recall in all these years past, but we once quarrelled over the best bait to use when fishing. If you can capitulate that worms are superior to squid bait, you may come for me at 11:00 a.m. Do not be tardy. C.

He found himself genuinely appreciating Charlotte's wit and tartness and did not delay with his response.

I will gladly capitulate as your company shall be far more stimulating than any fishing pole. I will call for you on the morrow, my fair lady. Yours, Adam.

Getting to his feet excited, he felt the most satisfied he ever had felt with a woman, which was laughable as he had not even taken her to bed. Still smiling, he planned out the rest of his day, wanting to while away the hours till tomorrow when he would be in her company.

The duchess, who would of course deny she was spying, was feeling very satisfied with her matchmaking as she passed the open door and caught Adam's rapt expression. *I*

will have grand babies in no time, she told herself smugly, as she continued her way down the hall.

Charlotte invited Emma, Harriet, and Eleanor for afternoon tea, and they were all eager to read the note the footman had brought her. Reading the note out loud, she could not contain either her blush or smug smile and her friends laughed and teased her mercifully.

"You will go down in ton history as a rogue tamer," exclaimed Eleanor. "He is smitten!"

"I would love to see the faces of those fortune-hungry title chasers when your betrothal is announced!" laughed Harriet.

"What beautiful babes you will make," Emma stated gleefully.

This comment brought an even deeper blush to Charlotte's face, and she could not help the unbidden thoughts of where their passionate encounters would lead. This also brought some doubt to her mind. Turning to her friends, who had simmered down seeing her sad and serious expression, she articulated her thoughts aloud.

"How can I truly know he has genuine intentions, with a reputation such as his? Will allowing his wooing only be to my detriment if it is a passing fancy?"

The ladies all looked at each other and after a few silent moments it was Emma, the most serious of all of them, who answered.

"His reputation, poor as it is, has never included dallying with the innocent debs like us. His mother, the duchess, also has a soft spot for you and he has made considerable effort in a short period suggesting a keen interest." Turning to the group, Emma asked, "What think you ladies?"

"I second what Emma states, Charlotte. He does look at you in the most besotted way. It is quite sweet," said Harriet.

"He is also very wealthy, so you need not worry it is your dowry either," Eleanor pointed out.

Satisfied with these responses, she relaxed, and butterflies fluttered in her stomach as the anticipation and excitement grew strong.

Over in Piccadilly, a carriage pulled up outside The Albany apartments. A widow dressed in a low-cut gown, slightly under the respectability of the ton standards, made her way to a footman dressed in the livery of the Viscount James Sheffield. The footman led Lady Adele to the Viscount's room where she was ushered into a library. Sheffield, who was sitting behind his desk, raised and gave a small bow and gestured for Lady Adele to take a seat. Sheffield sat back down.

"Your note intrigued me, my lady, requesting we meet to discuss business. I was not aware that we have any business."

Adele smiled seductively at the viscount, leaning forward slightly to draw his gaze to her cleavage. She felt triumphant when she saw his gaze did indeed travel. Adele loved nothing more than a man who could be led around by an appendage.

"Please let us drop any formality. You can call me Adele. I will call you James," she purred. "I wanted to discuss with you a mutual budding romance that would be in our better interests if it was squashed. And while we go about squashing it, we could enjoy a pleasurable and mutual benefit." She finished this statement with the opening and crossing of her legs.

James ran his eyes over Adele. He assumed she was in her early thirties, fair-skinned and voluptuous with thick black hair and eyes almost as dark. She screamed wanton.

Clearing his throat, James said, "Yes, let us drop the formality and call me James; however, I am confused as to what budding romance you speak of."

Laughing softly, hoping only she could hear the bitter undertone, Adele stood and sauntered over to the desk, perching herself on top and leaning closely into James's space.

"Let us not pretend we both did not see Langdon fawn over the Kentwell chit, the same chit you have been fawning over this season."

James went to interject, and she placed one finger against his lips to halt him.

"You are an attractive man with an attractive title, but the future duke is unmatched in seduction and could easily steal her affections. I can help to ensure he ends that pursuit, thus paving your own way to her heart."

James, slightly more at ease with the exchange and hearing the wisdom in her words, nodded.

"What do you gain from this? Langdon's own hand in marriage?" he asked.

In a bitter tone that she could not hide at all this time, she scowled at him.

"No. The future duke would never consider me for his future duchess, so all I seek is to make his life miserable."

Smiling widely at the daring woman in front of him, James grabbed her hips and pulled her closer, whispering against her lips.

"I am on board with whatever scheme you plot; however, I believe you mentioned mutual pleasures, so I would like to seal the deal first."

Adele opened her legs, slid forward into his lap and wrapped her legs around him, kissing him on the lips, while grabbing his hands to place each one on her breasts. That was all the encouragement and permission James needed. It was apparent that Adele was more than happy for him to swive her on the desk so, without any further pretence. James stood up and nudged her to lay down on the desk, pulling down her bodice. Adele knew she was generously proportioned and slyly laughed to herself that her breasts alone would keep him on the hook from the glint in his eyes. James caressed her breasts while sliding a hand up her leg. Adele purred out her encouragement and was pleasantly surprised. He was not as skilled as Adam, but he was not a fumbling idiot either and she began to enjoy his ministrations. As their passion took over, the plotting took a back seat. Fast and furious, they raced to find their own pleasure. Breathless, they sat there in silence until Adele spoke. "Consider the deal sealed. Now let's discuss my plan."

Chapter Eight

At precisely 9:50 a.m., Adam was waiting in the drawing room of Kent House being eyed suspiciously by Kentwell. He eyed the mantle clock as it slowly ticked over to 9:51 and wondered what to say. To ease the awkwardness, he was about to broach the topic of what breed of horses he had stabled when Kentwell abruptly asked, "What are your intentions towards my daughter? You have a terrible reputation, one of the worst in fact. Maybe amongst your friends you are revered but, as a father, you are the last suitor I want seated across from me."

He was taken aback by the duke's forthrightness. *Though it is now clear where Charlotte gets hers from*, he mused wryly.

He pondered his response for a few moments to ensure he chose the right words to impress what he hoped would be his future father-in-law.

"I understand your reservations, your grace. I daresay, if I am blessed with a daughter and found myself in your shoes, I would feel the same way. I do not deny my reputation nor apologise or make any excuses, but any man has a right to change, and it is usually due to the right woman. I believe that is your daughter."

Kentwell only grunted in response, but Adam could see his posture was slightly more relaxed. It was the longest and most meaningful speech he had ever made and all he received was a grunt. Nevertheless, he felt relieved and fought the urge to wipe the back of his hand against his forehead.

The next moment, his nostrils were tantalised by the scent of roses. He stood up quickly as she rushed in, dropped a curtsy and greeted him. He made his own bow, grasping her hand for a kiss, and was gratified by the blush that appeared on her cheeks. Behind Charlotte stood her ladies' maid, whom he hoped would act as chaperone since her aunt was nowhere in sight. A lucky start to the day.

She took the proffered arm he extended, and they both bid farewell to Kentwell, who graciously agreed to a two-hour picnic. As he assisted Charlotte into his barouche, he took the opportunity to scan his eyes appreciatively over her, her glossy hair covered in a straw bonnet with a pale green ribbon. Her promenade dress, the same pale-green material, moulded softly to the lush curves of her body. He assisted Macy as well and entered the barouche himself to sit opposite the two ladies. He caught Charlotte's eye and it was apparent his appraisal did not go unnoticed but, rather than catching her ire, he instead caught the sultry look in her own eyes. The idea his lust had raised her own caused him to grow hard in his breeches and he shook his head and tried to think of thoughts less arousing. Giving her one of his devilish grins, he instructed his driver to be on their way. With a swish of the reins, they started off on the journey to Hyde Park.

As always, Hyde Park was full of the ton, whether they

be riding, picnicking, or promenading, passing the time in the warm weather. He was intent on avoiding the gossip and stares, which they were even now drawing and advised the driver to angle the barouche down a path near the water, where he could leave the horses in comfort and find a secluded spot to lay the blanket and food he had brought along. Finding a good spot, he called a halt to the coachman and exited the barouche to go around to give Charlotte his hand to assist her descent. He assisted Macy as well but did not linger.

Charlotte watched as he turned back to the barouche and came back towards her with a blanket and basket. Macy requested to stay by the horses as she did not like water and Charlotte eyed her suspiciously, while Adam smiled. She knew this was a risky move, Macy giving her privacy, but she could not help but want it. He held the basket on one arm and proffered the other to Charlotte. They chose a spot of grass under the shade of a large tree, which also suited as shelter to prying eyes. Charlotte, suddenly filled with nerves, offered to serve the contents of the basket and brought out cheese, cold, roasted chicken, figs, bread, and wine, all the while feeling Adam's gaze roaming all over her. She felt as if someone had lit a match to her insides. Wanting to take the upper hand, she decided to strike up a conversation.

"It is a shame we do not have fishing poles; we could have proven my bait choice right."

"Was my capitulation not enough, my lady?" Adam replied with a bemused expression.

"Tell me, what other pastimes do you enjoy that we may share? Reading, fishing, what else?"

Charlotte, now sporting a mischievous grin, wondered how he would react to her many manly pursuits. That thought brought a little doubt, causing an unfamiliar pang of what she assumed was rejection by not meeting his standards. Her wilfulness pressed her on but could not contain the defensiveness of her tone, which Adam would surely notice.

"Well, my lord, if you must know, I am a very skilled rider and I enjoy racing, usually against the stable-hands back on the estate. I am an adept shooter and enjoy hunting and, though I only have my father to play with, he informs me I am a formidable billiards opponent." Charlotte waited with bated breath and prepared herself for masculine scorn but, instead, Adam threw his head back, his golden mane catching the sun while he laughed good-naturedly.

"You are so very surprising and unlike any woman I have met, and I say that with the highest of compliments. Let us dispense of the titled address; I am Adam and you are Charlotte." He drew her hand to his lips. She felt the softness of his lips graze her knuckles and raised her eyes to meet his.

"*If I be waspish, best beware my sting*" she quoted, curious for his response.

"Ahh, my sweet Charlotte, *no profit grows where is no pleasure ta'en*," he replied, grinning at her look of surprise.

"I spent yesterday catching up on my reading. Taming of the Shrew seemed like an appropriate choice, don't you think?"

She was unable to hold back the giggle at his impish smile and was elated he had made such an effort.

"Oh, Adam, you really are a charming devil, aren't you?"

Adam wondered how, whenever he found himself in her presence, he felt so at ease. No single woman had ever moved him to where he wanted to spend any time outside of the physical in their company. Adam did not believe he was quite capable of love after all his depravity and the countless married women he had bedded. Whatever the emotion he was feeling, it felt safe but frightening and confusing. He wanted to explore it further. He moved closer to her and cupped his hand on her cheek and spoke softly.

"I believe we may also enjoy another pursuit, Charlotte." He drew her face up to his to press his mouth to hers. Sensing her agreement, he applied more pressure, running his tongue across the seam of her lips until he heard her breath hitch and felt her lips part. Swiping his tongue along her bottom lip, he gently alternated at tugging her bottom and upper lip causing little sighs. His tongue swept into her mouth, sweeping in sensual circles until he felt her own tongue join his, not shy this time. Adam felt a hoarse breath escape, the kiss so untutored was still the most intoxicating, and he angled her head to the side so he could deepen their kiss.

She was swept up in the feelings he was awakening in her. She had never felt so alive and enraptured by another's touch. Her response was enthusiastic, and mayhap wanton, but she could not bring herself to care.

Sensing her passion, he could not control his next move. His free hand was drawn to cup her breast, he needed to fill the weight and shape of it in his palm. He heard her breath quicken and he moved his kisses down the elegant slope of her neck, giving little bites that he soothed with licks of his tongue. The breast he cupped was calling to him and she was subconsciously arching into him. He slipped his hand in her dress and pulled her chemise down, using his thumb to swipe across her nipple, which was already hard, tightened from her arousal.

She felt his roughened and calloused hands caressing her and it only enflamed her further. His hands were proof of the hardworking man he was, and not the stereotypical peer. Unable to hold back the growl that escaped him he was about to move her to lay down on the blanket to explore their passion further when voices broke through the lust pounding in his veins. With a curse, he released her and saw she was blushing furiously and righting herself. *What is it about him that makes me lose all good sense*, she thought, letting out an unladylike oath in her mind.

The voices faded and they sat there in silence for a few moments, both trying to calm pulses. She saw he was about to speak and, worried he would want to discuss their passionate encounter, she quickly spoke, asking about his estates. She saw his face light up as he began outlining a horse breeding program he was starting, which drew her own interest.

"I have a thoroughbred Arabian. Maybe you could use her? I have always wanted to foal her, as she is a real beauty."

He saw the genuine interest in her eyes and the feeling of contentment it gave him was so foreign. It truly amazed him how he found talking to her like talking to Lucas, Anthony or Jeremy. *Maybe this whole marriage deal won't be so bad.*

"I would like that. Breeding high-quality horses would combine a passion, pastime and profitable venture. It would be good if I had a partner," he said, hoping his voice didn't sound too eager. They continued to talk without pause until

Macy came to inform them it was time to make their leave home.

A niggling thought had entered Charlotte's mind as they left the park. As innocent as she was, she was no fool. Adam would have a high sexual drive but how could a man like him be satisfied during their courtship? Today was just an example of his lust. Was he still seeing other women? And what about marriage? Would it not be long before he grew tired of the marriage bed? She gazed at him as they made their way back to her home and she had the urge to slap the self-satisfied smirk off his face. He thinks I have already surrendered to his seduction!

Sensing her shifting mood, he turned to her but said nothing as they pulled in front of Kent House. Before he could get down to assist her, she hopped out of the barouche, caring naught for her manners. Giving him a cool 'thanks for today' with a small curtsy, she stared at him with a blank expression. He suppressed his annoyance at her sudden change in attitude and gave thanks back for her company. Watching her walk off, he could not help a few parting words.

"I will see you at the Clifford's ball tomorrow eve. Save me a waltz," he yelled to her retreating figure, flummoxed at her coolness.

Macy, who made her exit from the barouche with more decorum, allowing the driver to assist her, followed her mistress. Charlotte, in an unladylike manner, turned and called back over her shoulder, "We will see, Langdon," before disappearing inside.

Adam, frustrated and confused, advised the driver to make his way to Gentleman Jackson's. He planned to pummel his irritation away; the pugilistic establishment always helped cool his ire. He could not recall having someone frustrate him the way Charlotte did. *What was going on in that beautiful head of hers? Did we not just spend a pleasant day together? Women,* he shook his head. *No wonder I have been so content in bachelorhood.* He entered the establishment and saw Lucas already sparring in the ring. He felt his spirits rise since he and Lucas had a sparring routine that they always enjoyed. He yelled out while removing his jacket and waistcoat and rolled up his sleeves.

"Lucas, just the ugly face I needed to pummel out my frustrations on," he said, stepping into the ring.

The young man Lucas had been sparring with exited. Lucas, grinning at his disgruntled friend, replied with good-natured camaraderie, throwing his own insults back.

"Langdon, you coxcomb. You know you will never best me with those womanly punches you throw. Besides, you are too afraid to ruin your good looks to give it a real go!"

Grinning at their insults, they began to circle one another. Adam and his friends were all tall and on the larger side with well-honed muscles, but Lucas always seemed to be larger. They teased him about it being due to his heritage, likening him to a Viking of old with his ice blue eyes and fair almost-white hair to match. They proceeded with their boxing routine, not going easy on one another as the jabs and punches were thrown quick and fast.

After they had worn themselves out, they took a seat on the benches and opened a bottle of whiskey. Adam stared into his glass as he swirled the amber liquid in circles.

"What is on your mind, friend? You have not been yourself lately."

Appreciating his friend's direct approach, Adam just came out with it, glad not to have to put on any pretext.

"It's Charlotte," he sighed. "I am trying to court her, but she is so strong willed. I enjoy the chase, do not misunderstand, and I admire her strength and spirit. I just fear she will never see beyond my reputation and trust me."

Lucas checked his surprise. This was the first time he had seen Adam despondent over a woman.

"Adam, courting a young lady of her standing is not going to be quick, especially with her quick wit. Just be patient and give her no cause to think you will stray and, if you must stray, make sure you are very careful."

Disappointed but not surprised that even Lucas thought he could not be faithful, Adam just shook his head.

"That is the other problem. I have lost all desire for any other woman; she has gotten under my skin. I know I won't have her until I wed her, and I won't wed her till I convince her."

Seeing his friend in love caused Lucas a pang of envy and he started to ask Adam about the love he was feeling, but he was interrupted.

"Why do you think you have fallen in love...?"

"I am not in love with her. I just know she will be a perfect duchess and mother to my heirs. Plus, I will not tire of her. She is beautiful and clever, not like the other ladies, and she enjoys the same things as I. But I am not in love, come on, Lucas." He scowled at Lucas for suggesting as such.

Keeping a straight face at Adam's denials, he shrugged his shoulders and let the matter drop. Adam just did not yet realise that he was in fact in love. Throwing back the last of his drink, Lucas rose.

"Do not fret. Just keep using the season's opportunities

to bring her around. There is that ball tomorrow night and the following evening we have that Cyprian Ball for some distraction. A few good games of faro, some top-notch drink, and some very fine ladies to look at even if you aren't going to touch them. We will have you feeling yourself again." Lucas paused and then continued unable to resist a jibe.

"And you may as well enjoy yourself now before you go and leg shackle yourself."

He slapped Lucas on the back with brotherly affection, feeling better after getting his concerns off his chest, and nodded his agreement, except for the ladies part. He wanted to be committed to Charlotte. He would prove his worth.

Adam and Lucas had been so caught up in their deep conversation that they had not noticed another gentleman entering the establishment.

Chapter Nine

The Viscount James Sheffield could not believe his good luck. He rarely boxed, just every now and then to ensure he did not let himself go to paunch. He had sat hidden but within hearing distance to listen to that arrogant fop Langdon talk about his feelings for Charlotte. Adele's plan to ensure this love never blossomed between them was to turn them against each other. By her reasoning, Langdon was a proud man and, if Charlotte was to reject him, his pride would be crushed. After hearing Adam's talk, he saw Adele was right and, if he wanted Charlotte to himself, he had better follow any instruction Adele gave him.

Adele's plan for Charlotte was to ensure she held a low opinion of Adam as a suitor and husband. Adele had sneered at how Charlotte was prideful and wilful, turning her nose up at this and that. The viscount knew she was just jealous, but he had said nothing. Langdon could charm the skin off a snake so he knew he needed any interference he could get. She planned to spin stories that would get back to Charlotte's ears, affairs and such, to cause doubt. The Cyprian Ball thought Sheffield was just what he needed to get back to Charlotte. This news was of such import he did not even want to send Adele a note and decided to call on her instead. *And no doubt, this information would place Adele in a rather giving mood,* he thought, a salacious smile forming on his face.

The following evening the tension between Charlotte and Adam across the ballroom was palpable to their friends. They watched the stubborn pair attempting to ignore each other but anyone could see they were doing a poor job of it. Their friends wondered why there was such tension between the two and contemplated whether they should broach the subject, but the glowers coming from both their faces dissuaded them.

"It is going to be a long evening, my friends," Emma observed to Eleanor and Harriet, just as Lucas finished telling Anthony and Jeremy his own observation.

"Langdon is ripe for a fight tonight, best we keep him out of trouble."

Adam had had Freddy dress him in his usual black and white. Black pants, coat and shoes with a white shirt, silk waistcoat and cravat. All the other men had added the usual splash of colour, which only made him stand out more. His bronze tan, golden hair and emerald eyes were striking against the black and white backdrop of his large frame and he knew it. He noted Charlotte was dressed in shades of pink. The under layer of her gown was mauve, the top layer a light pink gauze, and it was all drawn in at her waist. From the waist down was another shade of pink, a soft rose, the sheer tulle shimmering as she moved. The feminine pinks emphasised her fair skin, violet eyes, and chestnut hair. *Damn her for looking so enticing*, he thought, casting angry looks her way.

And to infuriate him more, Sheffield was hanging off Charlotte. *Like he is courting her*, Adam thought darkly, watching his attentive movements. Sheffield made no secret of his designs on Charlotte and, to Adam's displeasure, she did not appear to be discouraging him.

Charlotte was brimming with fury as she continuously glanced over to Adam and Portia, who was batting her lashes and tittering behind her fan at everything he said. Everyone knew Portia was trying to wed Adam or one of his friends, but it was obvious that Adam was her preference. *And for someone who does not dally with innocent, young ladies, he appears to have changed his tune this season*, she thought contemptuously. I refuse to be in competition for his affections with a brainless twit! Sheffield held his hand out for their dance, and she accepted, turning her sight away from Adam.

Well, thought Adam, as he saw the pair go to dance, *Two can play at that game*. He had promised Lady Portia a waltz and, while waiting for the dance, she had not left his side, squeezing his arm, chatting incessantly. Her behaviour reminded him of an octopus, her arms clinging tentacles and cutting off the flow of blood in his arms. Extracting himself to talk to his friends, he moved closer to Anthony, who was staring at him, till Adam snapped.

"What are you staring at, Whitby?" he said, pulling Anthony aside, away from Portia's earshot.

"I am not sure. Where is the carefree rakehell we know and love? Tell us what is making you scowl. Is it Lady Charlotte?"

"Of course, it's Lady Charlotte. She makes a mockery over me, giving attention to that coxcomb Sheffield!"

"Come now. She is a pretty, fresh face. Lots of these fools will vie for her attention. It's harmless. I knew you fancied her, but I did not realise it was to this extent."

Adam turned to look at her again before replying in a frustrated tone.

"I am trying to bloody court the shrew, but she runs hot and cold!"

Anthony bit back his smile. He liked seeing Adam tied in knots over a woman.

"I must say though, Langdon, I am shocked you agreed to dance with Portia. Charlotte really must be under your skin if you are trying to make her jealous."

He agreed that had been rash. He regretted it already. Charlotte was the catch of the season but, unlike Adam, the likes of Sheffield and a few other gentlemen would fill their pockets if they gained a marriage with Charlotte. So why was she giving any of them the time of day. He did not know but he did know that he was not going to stand there much longer and tolerate it.

"Why don't you go over and request a dance?" suggested Anthony.

His green eyes turned dark in anger.

"And pry her out of Sheffield's fingers like a besotted fool? No."

With resignation, he turned his attention over to Portia; her incessant prattle could give anyone a distraction.

Charlotte's own jealousy piqued as she watched Adam throwing furious looks, so she threw them back. Insufferable fool! Her dance with Sheffield over and failing to notice his offence at how little attention she had paid him, she returned to her friends. Harriet the most sensitive of their group, had been watching the exchange and drew Charlotte to her, placing a comforting hand on her arm.

"Why don't you give the Marquess a smile and encourage him to come ask you for a dance? All the glowering he is doing suggests he is quite jealous over Sheffield."

She let out her usual unladylike snort.

"He seems more than happy to be leeched over by Portia. She has wrapped herself around him like the cravat on his neck."

How can he find us both attractive, when not solely basing it on looks? Portia is a willowy blonde, but her personality and mannerisms are totally different. I never act so missish or flirtatious! Maybe he wants that, and I am lacking. She began to worry. Scoffing at her moment of self-depreciation, she told herself to snap out of it. Turning her back on the spectacle again, she saw Sheffield had come back over.

"Is everything alright, my lady? You appear bothered by something or is it someone?" He inquired politely, wishing she paid him equal attention.

"I am perfectly well, but I thank you for your concern."

She paused and looked at him thoughtfully.

"You truly are a nice gentleman; did you know that?"

Sheffield just smiled, feeling slightly guilty with this deception and could not help grimacing inwardly. Yes, it was a nice compliment, but it did not sound like she held much affection for him, not as a potential husband anyway. Langdon had been throwing him dark glances all eve, so he must be doing something right. Determined to impress her with his charms, he touched his finger across her cheeks, under the guise of moving a stray strand of hair and complimented her beauty, hoping for a sign of interest, a blush, trembling. Charlotte cottoned on to his intent and willed herself to feel something, to prove Adam was not so special, but she felt nothing.

The duchess turned to her husband of thirty years with a large smile, pleased with her observations of her son and the woman she wanted him to marry.

"Can you feel the tension between Adam and Charlotte? Is it not wonderful observing their courtship?"

The duke stared at his wife with a lifted eyebrow, amused at her choice of words considering his own observations.

"Courtship? What I observe is outright warfare with those blazing looks."

Swatting her husband on the arm, she rolled her eyes and reminded him,

"You forget our own courtship, my love. We fought many skirmishes till we both called a truce."

Chuckling at the memories, he kissed his wife's cheek and murmured in her ear.

"Modest, my dear. You won the war. And I would not have had it any other way."

Lady Adele had also been observing the events unfolding. *That fool Sheffield certainly plays the lovesick fop to a tee,* she sneered. She was aware, however, after spending time within his company, it was wealth and luxury that motivated him, something this match would provide him with. But he was still smitten with her; she was just not a means to an end. But Adam, what a fool he was making of himself over this naive chit, who had probably no idea what truly went on between a man and woman. She knew firsthand the voracious sexual appetite Adam had and, whenever he married, it would not take long before he got himself a mistress. It made her jealous, more than she cared to admit when she noticed how intensely Adam watched Charlotte. It was the look of a man possessed, possessed with love? Or was it just lust? But the look on his face made her think that Charlotte was not another notch on his bedpost, unlike her. So bitter were her thoughts that Adele almost missed Charlotte and her group of wallflowers make their way in the direction of the women's tiring room, and she quickly left to follow. Catching Sheffield's eye, she gave a small nod that her plan was in action. It was time to perform, a role with which she was most comfortable.

The women's tiring room was fairly empty, and Charlotte and her friends found four chairs together. Before they could begin to talk, a woman entered in the most dramatic flair. The room itself smelt heavily of a mixture of perfumes that some of the ladies unfortunately doused themselves with.

"Less is sometimes more," muttered Charlotte, comparing her light scent of roses. Looking up, she saw it was Adele who had entered and spied some of her own friends. With a loud drawn out "Daarrliings," Adele made her way over to them. Rolling her eyes, as she heard Adele start to talk loudly, she had no choice but to hear what she had to say.

"Did you ladies hear there is a Cyprian Ball being held tomorrow night at Marlowe's establishment? I hear many of the ton are going, mainly the gentlemen, of course. I, myself, am going, the joys of widowhood."

As her friends giggled and encouraged her to tell them more, she did not hesitate.

"Yes, darlings. I will be attending and, of course, Langdon is going. Did I tell you I cut him off? I hope there will be enough women there for Langdon to chase after, as I, for one, have ended his pursuit of me. I could never settle for a man who treats woman so poorly. I hear at the last Cyprian Ball he was found alone, naked, with three women all at once. So, you can imagine exactly what was taking place."

As expected, Adele's friends gasped but in titillation rather than shock and made some bawdy comments of their own. The four young ladies' eyes widened at the remarks that were painting sullied images in their minds. A few older ladies thankfully entered the room, and Adele and her friends took their leave but not before Adele turned to Charlotte and gave her a malicious smile.

Emma, Harriet, and Eleanor were furious with Adele's antics and, seeing Charlotte's crestfallen expression, they immediately rallied to her side.

"Do not listen to that cow. Everyone knows she was only a passing fancy," Harriet angrily exclaimed. "And what is a Cyprian Ball anyway?"

"It is a party of immoral behaviour from what I understand," Eleanor answered with a blush.

"What kind of lady even promotes that she attends these parties in that manner? She is certainly no lady," stated Emma crossly, who had had brief interactions as Adele was a friend of her stepmother. Eleanor hugged Charlotte.

"I do not trust anything that comes from that viper's mouth. Jealousy really does embitter a person." Grateful for her friends' support, Charlotte did hear the wisdom in their words.

"It may have all been exaggerated ill humour but that does not mean Adam will not attend tomorrow night and, if he does, he is only a man and I highly doubt he will forgo pleasures of the flesh, even if he means to truly court me."

None of them had experience in these matters and were unsure of what to say. She couldn't sit here though and be played a fool and then it hit her. They were now alone in the room, but she still whispered, her idea so risqué.

"I know! I will spy on him! These balls are masquerades, are they not? I can disguise myself and see his behaviour for myself."

There was a stunned pause then they all started talking at once, but to everyone's shock the most level-headed and sensible one of the group turned to Charlotte.

"I will go with you," Emma said firmly.

Charlotte immediately rejected the offer, but Emma insisted this was not one she should go alone. Eleanor and Harriet looked at each other, stating in unison, "We are in as well."

Emma reminded them both they had families that may be harder to sneak away from.

"We need to be aware of the risk. If we are caught, that will be the end of us in polite society. We would never recover from the scandal. But, hell, I have never fit in anyway," she said with an unladylike snort.

They laughed giddily as the implications sunk in. Emma reassured her they would succeed and set out to discuss the plan logically.

"We must get in, complete our mission and get out undetected."

Each lady imagined with horror the backlash that would occur should Emma and Charlotte be discovered.

The ladies sat in the tiring room for a while longer and, in hushed tones, laid out the details. She would stay over at Emma's, as her father was away, and her stepmother cared naught for her. The servants were loyal to Emma and would say nothing. Emma advised there were masks put away from previous masked balls and there were old clothes in the attic they could don as costumes.

As they returned to the ballroom, she realised Adam was no longer there. But Portia was and looked very sulky mused Charlotte with satisfaction. Buoyed with her plan, she told herself she would give Adam this opportunity to prove to her he could give up his rakish ways. *If he does not want to, then he can cease his courtship and cease wasting my time,* she told herself sternly. Finding her aunt, she requested they leave; she had plans to go over. If Aunt Anne knew, she could imagine the reprimand now: *"Young ladies do not attend establishments of ill repute."*

Chapter Ten

Adam had left the ball, mad at Charlotte, mad at himself, and mad at Sheffield. He cursed his luck in developing feelings after all these carefree years. Jeremy left with him and suggested they drink elsewhere and play a few hands of cards. Adam agreed, not because he particularly felt like doing so, but because his other options were to stay at the ball and become further enraged or to go home and brood in silence. At least the cards would distract him and the drink would numb the pain. *Pain? Yes, pain,* he thought. *This feeling eating away at me like a lovesick fool is pain at the thought of Charlotte choosing another over me.* Disgusted with himself, he threw his arm around his friend's shoulders.

"Let us drink till we see the sun come up and play cards till our pockets are empty or too full to hold anymore winnings."

And that, Adam thought, *is what happens when a rogue takes one step forward; he takes two steps back.*

The following evening, Adam, Lucas, Anthony, and Jeremy entered the Cyprian Ball. It was a debauched affair held annually for the elite of the ton and could go for days. Strong alcohol and decadent food flowed freely, courtesans were all welcoming and all kinds of depravity catered for. They all wore black domino masks and informal outfits of black breeches and white shirts, cravats loose and their sleeves rolled up. They looked identical if not for their different hair colour. Adam and his friends greeted the host, Mr Caldwell, with their tickets. He charged an exorbitant fee for entry to these gatherings but, in exchange, offered precious anonymity to those more discreet members of the peerage.

It was not even 10:00 pm but the depravity was in full swing in the dimmed room. Men and women were scantily dressed, some in lewd positions and all with no shame. Jeremy farewelled his friends when he saw an old flame. Laughing, Adam, Lucas and Anthony made their way through the crowds and several women, a mix of courtesan and ladies in disguise, beckoned them. They soon lost Anthony to the temptation of two hedonistic women who appeared to be of the courtesan persuasion.

Lucas, concerned for Adam who was still not back to his jovial state of mind, followed him but stopped as they were halted by a sultry female clad in an almost see-through black gown and glittering black mask.

"Good evening, my Marquess of Sunderland. Can I tempt you into sharing a drink with me?" purred a voice belonging to Adele. Brusquely, Adam walked past her, not even pretending to be courteous.

"Not now. I am looking for a card game only this evening."

Lucas caught the outraged expression on her face, and he gave a slight bow to the seething Adele, going after Adam. When he caught up to him, he gave him sound advice to be on guard with Adele.

"There is nothing like a woman scorned, old friend."

Adam snorted in derision.

"Scorned? For what? I made no such promises to that woman. She has bedded half the ton. I should be no different."

Noting he was being dismissive to his friend, he added with a sheepish grin, "But I appreciate the advice and your concern. Truly, my friend, you can go enjoy yourself. I am not in such a black mood that I will gamble my fortune away."

Lucas waved him off, not insulted at all.

"I will play a few hands at the opposite table. Your faro skills, black mood or not, never seem to go against you. I will enjoy a few rounds before I find a saucy wench to enjoy," Lucas said with a wicked smile.

Seating themselves at the respective tables, Adam signalled for a drink and laid out his bet, ready to cease all thoughts of a violet-eyed beauty he worried would never be his.

The unmarked carriage Emma's footman had arranged pulled up outside the Cyprian Ball, held in an inconspicuous building in Cheapside. Taking one last look at each other, Emma and Charlotte exited the carriage. Emma informed the footman to have the driver wait for them in the alley and he to wait outside to escort them back once they were done. Emma had elected to wear a light blue silky gown, the material light and flowing showing off her petite figure but still modest around her bust, the neckline not dipping too low. Over her face, she wore a silver mask that was adorned with diamantes. The combination of the glittering silver and pale blue silk contrasted beautifully against her bluebell-hued eyes and strawberry blonde curls, which were pulled back, with loose curls framing her face. Charlotte had also dressed alluringly but modestly, as could be managed. Her white silky gown was trimmed with lace, the dress flowing off her curves sensually. A demi-mask of white satin and white feathers upon her face and her dark glossy hair loose, an enticing contrast to the white. Charlotte knew it was unseemly for a lady to wear her hair this way, but she also figured that tonight her role was to not be recognised as a lady. The doorman, checking their invites that Emma had somehow procured, held open the door and a servant ushered them down a long dark corridor where another door was opened. Their innocence flew out the door as it closed behind them.

Charlotte and Emma crossed the threshold, and the scent of strong incense assailed their senses. Charlotte inhaled the overwhelming scent of sandalwood and jasmine. They were instantaneously shocked by the scene that greeted them as they looked around the dimly lit room and for a moment both girls wanted to flee as they tightly clutched hands. Before them were scenes they had never even thought to imagine. Women and men, in all stages of undress and *flagrante delicto*.

"Was that Viscount Whitby?" she whispered to Emma, squinting her eyes at a man with a woman seated on each thigh. Thankful for the masks that covered most of their flaming blushes, they slowly edged their way around the room. A servant handed them drinks and, as they sipped, they realised these drinks were far more potent than the ratafia they usually had at their normal social gatherings.

Trying to keep their eyes averted from the debauched scenes but still trying to identify if any of these men may be Adam, they scanned the crowd.

"I think we are getting attention," Emma whispered to her.

Without warning, a burly man stepped in between them, grabbed both their arms and made a lewd suggestion. Emma thought the voice sounded like Lord Percy and was disgusted a gentleman would behave in such a manner. She glanced at Charlotte, who also looked disgusted, and questioned with her eyes what they would do to be rid of the man without revealing their identities. Clearly these gatherings were running under a rule of implied consent. They had not anticipated the current predicament they found themselves in when making their plans.

Across the room, Lucas was watching. He had enjoyed his rounds of cards and the attention of a saucy redhead who was eagerly brushing herself up against him. The flurry of interest that captured some of the men had distracted him though, and he had looked up to see the object of their interest. *Two females, angelic and sweet looking,* he had mused, *compared to all the devilment around him.* He had noted they were edging their way around the room like they were on a mission, but not a mission for pleasure, and he sensed their alarm. Lucas now saw Percy saunter over to the women and lay his claim to them both. The two women looked anything but pleased and had stiffened with his approach. As Lucas stepped a little closer, he noted the women were petite, the strawberry blonde would just come up to his chin. He had seen this shade before he pondered to himself. The dark-haired woman also seemed familiar. Stroking his chin after careful further observation, he wondered why it was they both looked familiar. Then to his astonishment, when the pair turned at the same time, he saw a pair of eyes like bluebells and a pair of purple-hued eyes, and he cursed out loud. "Bloody hell, Christ." It was Lady Emma and Lady Charlotte.

Making his way over to them, he quickly interceded as Emma looked ready to punch Percy in the nose, while Charlotte's knee was slightly raised and poised to knee Percy in the bollocks.

"Sorry, old friend. These women already have a prior appointment with me but, not to worry, there is a saucy redhead over there who will be amenable to your charms," Lucas declared while removing Percy's hands from the women.

Thankfully, Percy, who had always been a good-natured drunk, put up no fight, only calling Lucas a lucky bastard before giving up the women. His strength enabled Lucas to pick up a lady under each of his arms and he walked off to find a private room, cheers following him. The bundles under his arms were wriggling in outrage.

As soon as he found an empty room, he unceremoniously dropped the ladies, who had not yet realised Lucas knew their identity, and all three began to yell at once.

"How dare you manhandle us, you uncouth cur," began Emma.

"Touch us again and I will knee your bollocks into your throat," Charlotte viciously spat, but it was Lucas's bellow of, "What the bloody hell are two innocent ladies of your standing doing coming to a bloody den of inequity," that stopped them short in their tirade.

Charlotte stared at him open-mouthed and speechless and only Emma found her voice to say, "You know who we are."

"Yes!" roared Lucas. "Lady Emma and Lady Charlotte, I am not blind nor drunk off my tit as the men are back in there," realising his coarse language, Lucas began to apologise and Emma cut him off.

"I never realised you even knew who I was. It is my second season out and you have never even acknowledged me."

Lucas started at her bold and truthful statement. He realised that, while it may have seemed that way, he had noticed more than he was aware of to have recognised her in this disguise and by her eyes. As he raked his glance over from head to toe, he saw just how stunning she was. Emma felt herself become warm under his appraisal and gave her own one back, causing Lucas to feel not only physically naked but also emotionally. He shook his head, trying to free himself of such thoughts.

Charlotte, watching this exchange and feeling like an interloper, cleared her throat.

"Thank you for your rescue, my lord. We are in your debt. We now see our plan was flawed and, if you can assist in escorting us out unseen, we would be eternally grateful."

Lucas shook his head.

"First, my ladies, please pray tell, what are you two even doing here?" he asked, trying to keep his voice even. The women looked at each other and seemed embarrassed and hesitant to answer. The answer dawned on him, and he threw his hands up in the air in realisation.

"You are spying on Langdon!" he groaned.

Charlotte instantly became defensive, tossing her head upwards in defiance.

"Do you deny he is here and involving himself in the debauchery we saw? Now I think on it, I believe we saw your friend Lord Whitby indulging himself."

Lucas, ignoring the latter, cleared his throat.

"I can assure you the Marquess is in the same spot he has been since we arrived, playing cards, and now I must go fetch him otherwise it will be my neck on the line." Charlotte paled.

"Please do not tell him. I am mortified enough."

Shaking his head, Lucas replied, "My lady, I can ensure your safety, your way home unseen, but I will not keep this from my closest friend who, believe it or not, does have tender feelings for you. Bar this door after I leave and do not open it until you hear my voice. There are people here that will recognise you and it isn't just men here. I have seen Adele and a few other ladies, so stay here." With that stern warning, he left.

Charlotte and Emma did as he asked and locked the door and sat on the bed in silence both too flummoxed to speak.

Lucas made his way to the gaming room wondering what to say to Adam. He decided it would be best just to show him. Adam was just about to play another round when Lucas whispered.

"I need you to come with me now."

Adam followed without question, only asking Lucas what was wrong. Lucas just shook his head and led him to a door, giving it a firm knock.

"Open up. It's Lucas."

The door opened and Adam saw two women staring back to him, a little blonde and a tempting brunette. In his inebriated state of mind, he thought, *Has Lucas found me a clone of Charlotte?* Squinting at her, he thought, *Even her lavender eyes are the same.* As he stepped closer, he thought, *Even the stubborn set to her jaw.* The white dress and mask made her look like an angel. A debauched angel that was narrowing her eyes at him in warning. It dawned on him.

"Bloody hell, Charlotte. What are you doing here?" he bellowed across the room.

All at once, everyone in the room started yelling for the second time that night. Adam saw a privacy screen in the corner of the room and dragged Charlotte behind it. Clutching his hands in her face, he whispered fiercely, "What are you doing in a place like this?"

Charlotte decided she would just be honest and whispered back, "Spying on you."

"How did you even know I would be here?" he asked, incredulous.

"I heard your mistress, Adele, discussing it loudly last night," she said, her tone challenging.

"Bloody hell, Charlotte. She isn't my mistress. I want nothing to do with her and have made it clear. The only woman I want is you. Just you," he said, hating the pleading tone in his voice. She heard it as well and placed her small hands in his large warm ones.

"I want you as well, Adam." Her tone was now shy admitting something so personal.

With a groan, Adam pulled her against him, tore of their masks and gave her a hard, punishing kiss. She had experienced several of his kisses but this one curled her toes. It was forceful but tender. She could feel the fright she had given him and his concern all in his kiss.

Emma blushed and Lucas felt awkward. They could not look at each other when hearing the kissing sounds coming from behind the screen. *Damn*, thought Lucas, *Why am I acting like a nervous pup? I have enough experience with women.* Sneaking a peak at Emma's face, he thought, *But never have I been with someone so sweet, someone most likely never been kissed,* and he felt a tug pull on his heart strings.

He called to Adam to avoid the questions racing through his mind and the awkward situation.

"I think you should save your making up for a different time, old friend. We need to get the ladies out of here."

Adam removed his mouth from Charlotte's, and they were both breathless as they stared intensely into each other's eyes.

"He is right. I am still furious, and we will talk about this later. Your distrust of me has placed you in a dangerous position, and your friend as well. Dammit, Charlotte, you need to give me a proper chance."

Feeling chastised, she nodded, the enormity of the situation dawning on her. Donning their masks, he held Charlotte tightly under one arm, ordering her to keep her face turned to his chest and Lucas did the same with Emma. Once outside Emma led them to her footman who led them to the carriage. Lucas assisted Emma into the carriage, and she assured Lucas and Adam both servants were loyal to her. Lucas still felt a protective need to threaten the servants with bodily harm if this news ever got out and they both agreed on their lives that would never happen. Adam said he would call on her for a ride soon, so they could have a serious talk, before stealing a final kiss.

Emma and Charlotte made their way back to Emma's home, laughing as the nervous tension ebbed, but nothing was funny. They were filled with questions they were not ready to hear themselves say out loud. As they got into bed, the initial plan to have a sleepover and gossip all night seemed childish, and they were both silent. Charlotte was reliving Adam's kisses, while Emma could not help but wonder how Lucas's would feel.

Chapter Eleven

Over at Emma's home the next morning, four young ladies were having an extremely scandalous conversation in hushed tones in the drawing room. Charlotte and Emma regaled Eleanor and Harriet in excruciating detail the events of their adventure the evening past. No detail was left out except that Charlotte did not mention her kisses with Adam and Emma omitted the new *tendre* she was feeling for Lucas. It was not that they did not trust their friends; they had discussed their own emotions on these situations before they had arrived.

Eleanor and Harriet's eyes grew as round as saucers when they were described the debauched scenes they had witnessed. Just listening to the taboo retelling caused each of them to blush. In an attempt to steer the direction of their unladylike thoughts, it was Harriet who asked the probing question.

"What are your feelings now, Charlotte? You didn't catch Langdon in the act and, from what you have told, he was content to play cards all night. Even the Earl of Chester informed you of his feelings for you."

Charlotte caught Emma's blush at the mention of Lucas's title.

She knew she had to make a choice. Her heart was saying yes but her head was still holding her back, for fear of making a mistake. But she knew if she did not take this chance, she would regret it. She took a deep breath and addressed her friends with her decision.

"I am going to give him a chance and my heart too. I am scared but I do not want to live with regrets. The way he makes me feel, and I know he does care for me, it makes his reputation pale in comparison."

Eleanor clasped her hands against her chest and made an excited noise. Harriet reached over and squeezed her hand. Emma caught her eye, gave her a smile and nodded her head, as she had seen firsthand the connection between them.

Over on St James's Street, a little later that same day, Adam, Lucas, Anthony, and Jeremy were seated in a corner of White's, speaking in low tones. The topic was also the night before. Cigar smoke and the combined smells of whiskey and brandy permeated the air. The other gents in residence talked loudly over cards, giving them enough cover to have their risqué conversation.

Anthony and Jeremy were stunned with what Adam and Lucas were saying. Emma and Charlotte had been at the Cyprian Ball? Anthony also had the decency to blush when it was mentioned the ladies had even recognised him.

"Of course, the one night I indulge, I am the one to be

ousted," he said, throwing his hands up in the air, and they all laughed.

Jeremy, concerned, asked, "Are you sure that nobody knew they were there? Even Percy is not that daft, drunk or not?"

Adam shook his head and took a big drink of his whiskey, unsure what to think, the brown liquid burning a trail down his throat. It was Lucas who raised a valid point.

"Even if he was suspicious, he will never be able to prove it, nor would anyone believe it. I would make it clear that I would call him out at dawn if he tried to impugn their honour."

Anthony and Jeremy were surprised at the threatening tone in Lucas's voice and looked to Adam.

"Yes, gents, it appears I am not the only one stung by Cupid's arrow," said Adam, now laughing. The serious mood lifted as Anthony and Jeremy stared in shock at Lucas.

Scowling in an attempt to cover his blush, Lucas replied in a gruff tone, "I have not been struck by any arrow, but Lady Emma is an innocent little lady and would not deserve any taint on her name." He smiled fondly at the thought of her. "Aye, she is a little lady but courageous. She looked ready to plant one in Percy's face. You would think she trains over at Jack's."

They all laughed, and Adam admitted to his friends that, as well as the events had turned out, the fear he felt when he saw Charlotte clad like a wanton and propensity for the danger it may bring was unlike anything else he had ever felt for a person. Yes, he was angry, and, yes, a little lustful when he had taken in her appearance, but all he wanted to do was protect her from any harm.

"Those are some very strong feelings, Langdon," Anthony said, whistling under his breath. "So, this is love?"

Usually when the word love was raised, he went on the defensive, but this time he didn't. Before his friends could delve deeper, he stood up, informing them he was going to meet with Charlotte tomorrow and needed time to think.

His friends watched him leave and Jeremy looked to Lucas and Anthony, "One down and three to go, or two," he said, giving Lucas a wink.

Anthony laughed and Lucas felt that blush creep up and scowled, "Sod off, you lot."

Adam called at Kent House the following day to take Charlotte for a ride and again found himself sitting opposite Kentwell. However, this time he noted Kentwell's greeting was a little more cordial and they passed the few minutes amicably discussing Adam's plan for his horse breeding program. The idea had piqued Kentwell's interest, and he was telling Adam of his close friendship with Richard Tattersall while pouring him a brandy. Adam was about to take another sip but was glad he didn't, as he would have spat it out in surprise.

Charlotte came into the room dressed in a riding habit, but this was no ordinary riding habit. She wore a tailored jacket over fitted breeches and a skirt covering her thighs to her knee. It was highly erotic and like nothing he had seen before.

Charlotte, catching his glance, blushed, "I know it is considered unladylike to ride astride but, after my years in the country with no need to ride side saddle, I simply cannot bear to ride unless I am astride, and this outfit allows me to do so."

She was proud of her riding habit, having designed it herself, and she wanted Adam's approval to prove to her he accepted all her non-societal norms.

Adam, remembering Kentwell was close by and suspected the stare he was giving her was bordering lecherous, quickly schooled his features. He was unable to mask the adoration in his tone when he heard himself talk.

"I think you look marvellous and riding astride means I won't have to reduce my pace for you. And I praise your talent in design, my lady." His genuine smile warmed her heart.

But at these words, a challenge gleamed in her.

"I warn you now, my Lord, my Cleo can outstrip most stallions, so be cautious if you intend to throw out a challenge." Kentwell laughed.

"Now, now, no racing through Hyde Park. The ton will have an apoplexy enough over your attire," he said, turning to Adam.

"Charlotte's maid does not ride and her Aunt is not up for riding so I have asked two of the footmen to chaperone."

Thanking Kentwell, he gave assurance he would have her back by 4:00 p.m. and was given another shock.

"No rush, my boy, and you are welcome to stay on and partake in our evening meal." Giving a final bow, amazed at his good luck, he escorted her outside.

"You have certainly impressed father. What did you say?"

Bemused, Adam replied, "I haven't the faintest idea." But, whatever the reason, he was glad.

Adam took in the magnificent creature Charlotte sat astride, chestnut with white markings, but no sight could be any more magnificent than Charlotte herself. Tapering down his enthusiasm, he mounted Argo and drew close.

"Once we reach privacy in the park, we must discuss the Cyprian Ball. I am still furious with the danger you put yourself in. Will your footman allow it?"

Biting the inside of her cheek, her lavender eyes flashing with a combination of regret and defiance when remembering the purpose of this ride.

"Yes, Charlie is Macy's beau, and she has told him to heed my instructions, even if I request to be alone with you, and the other footman will agree." She paused and gave him a cheeky smile.

"They also know I can defend myself with a swift knee to the bollocks."

On that note, she hurried Cleo forward. *The cheek of this woman,* he thought, but quickly corrected himself, *No, not this woman, my woman,* and rode after her. He chose a less conspicuous route and path to avoid the ton's prying eyes and was glad the day was overcast meaning less people around. A few people stared at Charlotte's attire oddly but that was a given.

When they arrived, Adam led her on foot along a less popular trail that was overgrown and through a copse of trees, leaving Charlie with the horses. Adam assisted her to the ground so they could face each other in a seated position. She saw his face turn serious and knew he was about to raise her impulsive decision to follow him to the Cyprian Ball and braced herself. He took a deep breath, damning the nerves he felt.

"We need to discuss your feelings towards me. I believe you want my suit otherwise we would not be sitting here but for this to work we need trust, Charlotte. The danger you put yourself in, not just your reputation, but physically?

Some of those men, even women, are absolute animals in those situations. If you cannot bring yourself to trust me, I fear we cannot continue with one another."

Saying the words out loud, he felt a pain across his chest and held his breath waiting for her to speak, worried she may walk away from him. His palms grew sweaty as he watched her eyes moved down to stare at the grass.

Just before the silence became unbearable Charlotte spoke, her voice faltering slightly as she lifted her face to meet his eyes.

"I will trust you. I do trust you. I will open my heart to you and accept you as you are, and I want you to accept me as I am as well."

"Oh, sweetheart, it has never bothered me that you are not the ton's expectation of a lady. In fact, that's what makes me want you even more. You have lit a fire in my heart I never thought I would feel. I want to marry you."

All she could do was nod, not accustomed to the emotion welling inside her, and that was answer enough.

Pulling her towards him, words done, he gently leaned her back onto the grass and kissed her, watching her lashes flutter and close over her beautiful eyes. She reached her hands up and thread them through his golden mane and pulled him close, their mouths now parted and kissing one another in reckless abandon. Her motion to pull him closer caused his weight to settle on her and, rather than feeling cumbersome, it further aroused her passion. They pressed their bodies into one another, equally marvelling at how perfect their bodies fit. Soft curves against hard muscle.

Adam, cupping her head with one hand, moved his kisses across her cheek, to the slope of her neck where he nipped sensually and began a path of warm kisses from behind her ear down to her decolletage. Charlotte squirmed underneath him making soft noises of encouragement and he used his free hand to sweep down the curves of her body and feel her lush breasts and the womanly curves of her waist and hips. He swept this hand back up to cup her breast and lifted his head to watch her face. Her expression caused him to harden even more as he stared into her eyes, which were hooded and darkened with desire. He moved his thumb across her nipple and felt her tremble. She was stunned that this slight touch caused her to tingle. He opened her jacket and dipped his head to lick her nipple through the soft linen of her garment underneath. She cried out and clutched his head tighter to her breast and this was all the incentive he needed to unbutton her garment and pull her chemise down to look upon her breasts. In this moment, she truly cared nothing for proprietary or society, instead she felt all lustful woman when she saw the awe and craving on his face.

He took in the two white mounds. They were perfect as he cupped their shape and delighted with how they filled his hands, her nipples dusty pink rose, hard and tight with desire.

"I need to taste you, Charlotte," he said, his voice husky with lust. He dipped his head again taking a nipple in his mouth, swirling his tongue around its peak. Charlotte, so impassioned, began to rub her lower self against him, causing Adam to growl in satisfaction and he sucked her nipple harder. As much as he wanted to take her, this moment needed to be about Charlotte and the pleasure he could bring her. He could wait till they were married he told himself. He moved to her other breast, as she was clearly enjoying his ministrations, and slid his hand down her breeches, feeling the warmth emanating from her arousal, noting she wore no drawers. *How interesting*, he thought, *to slip my hand into breeches and not up a skirt.*

He cupped the essence that made her all woman and she pressed into him, encouraging him to tantalise her further. He parted her tenderly and felt her wetness, gliding his fingers against her gently and looking for the centre of her pleasure, massaging it until he felt her quiver. Their eyes caught and the intimacy of the moment intensified. Using one finger, he gently slipped it into her, causing a gasp. The dual assault of his thumb and finger, rubbing and thrusting, made her arch her hips.

Charlotte felt like she was on fire, exquisite fire. The sensations he was drawing from her breasts and her feminine core were making her gasp and shake and she did not know whether to beg him continue or pray he stop. It did not take Adam long with all his skills to make Charlotte's body tense, his skilled fingers firm and sure quickly bringing her to climax. Her body tensed and felt like she could not breathe but, all at once, the most amazing feeling she had ever experienced spread throughout her entire body, all her nerves tingling. He heard her cry out and lifted his head to watch the expression on her face as she let go and the beauty of it made him forget his own painful, aching arousal.

In the back of her mind, she knew she should be embarrassed by her wanton behaviour but, with the way Adam looked at her with such awe and adoration, she could not feel any regrets. What she could feel though was Adam's hardened desire pressed against her and, on instinct, she reached her hand down to stroke the long length through his breeches. He closed his eyes and let out a ragged breath, all his good intentions went astray as he grabbed her in a hungry kiss and undid his breeches, pulling her hand inside and encouraged her to wrap her hand around his hard erection. She needed no encouragement and whispered huskily, "Show me what to do so I can bring you the pleasure you gave me."

Adam laid his hand over her own and guided her in a grip he enjoyed and the strokes he desired to reach his peak. She enjoyed his moans and shudders that wracked his body, exhilarated she was the cause. He kept kissing her until he felt himself about to climax and moved his face into her neck and yelled out an oath as he erupted. They both laid there spent, still breathing heavily, just staring into each other's eyes. His eyes betrayed the emotion she knew was mirrored in her own after sharing such an intimate moment.

"Is it always like this?" Charlotte whispered shyly, these feelings new to her.

"No," he said, kissing her forehead. "It is not but, for you and me, it always will be."

Chapter Twelve

They laid content in each other's arms, hidden away in this copse of trees, and discussed their future. Stroking her cheek as he watched her animated face talk, he had never felt such peace before.

"You know I love to garden, Adam, especially roses. I will need to start a plot when we move to your estate, after we marry," she murmured dreamily.

"You can have anything you want, my sweet. I cannot wait to show you the grounds at Hallend," he said, pressing soft kisses to her hands.

"Will you miss cavorting around town as a depraved bachelor?" she asked in an impish tone.

"You know, I am actually looking forward to nights spent cuddled in front of the fire reading. Or playing billiards but, I warn you, I will not let you win," he replied, matching her tone.

"Well, I do not want to show you up too much, my handsome marquess, so I may let you win now and again," she said, returning his kisses.

They realised it was getting late and Kentwell had

invited him for dinner. Adam advised her he would ask her father for his permission and blessing for a betrothal tonight.

Charlotte, upon entry, quickly went upstairs to change and make sure there was no telling sign of what had transpired between them. While Charlotte was upstairs, Adam asked Kentwell formally for Charlotte's hand.

"Your Grace, I want your permission to take Lady Charlotte's hand in marriage," he said, posing it as a statement instead of a question.

He felt a nervous, clammy-like sweat begin to develop on his skin as he waited for the answer when it occurred to him that Kentwell may refuse.

"You have my blessing, son. In respect to the dowry ...," but Adam held up a hand to interject. "I have no questions or concerns. Let us not worry over those details and let's just break bread," he said, his charming smile plastered back on his face, mixed with relief over the acceptance.

Kentwell broke out a bottle and, as they shared a brandy, Adam started to feel the reality set in. He is getting leg shackled voluntarily and he could hardly wait!

Dinner was an amicable affair, the talk easy between them and Aunt Anne who had joined them, ecstatic over the news. She had let out her own very unladylike, "I knew it!" They all laughed when Charlotte said, "Ladies do not yell in front of company."

Charlotte learned more about Adam as he spoke with her father and recalled the duchess had told her similar. It still impressed her how diligently he worked, unlike other lords who took their lands for granted. He explained how he spent time with his tenants, working the land. It was so uncommon for one of the peerage and she was proud of him. He and her father also shared similar views on agricultural and tenant rights and, when she offered her own thoughts, he beamed with pride of his own, happy in the knowledge he was wedding an equal and not a vapid lady who would spend her day shopping and gossiping. Adam advised he would arrange dinner with his parents before they announced any formal engagement and they all agreed.

Two people, who would not be happy to learn of this suit, laid together half undressed in bed. The bed belonged to the Viscount James Sheffield and his accomplice Lady Adele. Adele thought it would be best to bed Sheffield before she told him her plan. She was still seething at being spurned at the Cyprian Ball. Adele realised the events so far were not the right setting for what she had in mind and, realising Charlotte was friends with the Countess of Moreland's stepdaughter Emma, she had developed a diabolical plan. She would simply have to ensure Charlotte was caught in the act of betraying Adam.

Casually, she started, "I am going to engage my dear friend, Louise, the Countess of Moreland, to hold a weekend at her country house and Emma her stepdaughter, who is friends with Charlotte, will invite her and I will ensure you and Langdon are also invited." Sheffield slightly nodded but kept quiet and she continued.

"We will arrange a meeting with you and Charlotte,

and I will also send a note to Langdon. All you have to ensure is that she is caught in your embrace when he walks in, believing she has sent for him to meet her."

Sheffield looked slightly shocked but did not knock her plan back. Sheffield pondered it for a moment before he replied.

"I do not want her compromised or any scandal attached. Can you ensure only Adam will see?" Adele assured him she could.

"Trust me, as soon as Langdon sees he is being played for a fool by the silly chit, he will turn his back on her suit, and you will be the only object in her affections."

Sheffield shrugged, stating he would leave it in her hands. Adele laid her head back on the pillow, satisfied that this plan will result in that heartless bastard, Adam, feeling the sting of love's prickled thorns.

Charlotte was working in her rose garden the following morning, lost in thoughts of the previous day's events. The feel of fresh soil and dirt beneath her hands always made her feel grounded. The feeling of contentment was still present, as was her ridiculously large smile. The passion and pleasure Adam made her feel physically was more than she ever imagined possible. The idea of any other men touching her made her shudder with distaste. And her most favourite part was his acceptance of her. Daydreaming, she began to think of children. They would be responsible for two future dukes. Smiling, she imagined of all Adam would teach them. Lost in the familiar routine of pruning her roses and her thoughts of her future with Adam, she did not hear footsteps approach.

"Hello, love." Her father's voice broke through her musings. "You have been out here for a while. It is almost luncheon." Charlotte stood and stretched her back. She had been stooped over for longer than she realised.

"Father, how did you know when you were in love with mother?"

Kentwell's face, as always when the duchess was mentioned, took on a bittersweet look.

"I thought I did as soon as I laid eyes on her but, when shortly after I heard her laugh, it struck something deep inside me and I knew I would love her for all my days."

Shaking his head as if trying not to get lost in his melancholy thoughts, he focused back on Charlotte. "Are you questioning your feelings, dearest?" It was now time for Charlotte to shake her own head.

"No. I do not know what I am feeling but I trust and respect Adam and find him very handsome," she admitted with a blush, "And I could not imagine being with anyone else." Chuckling at her sudden shyness, he took her arm to help her stand and she rubbed her dirty hands on her apron.

"It does sound like you are falling in love but do not over think it. Allow the feelings to grow, and nature will take its course. I must admit, I did hold reservations; no father wants their daughter swept away by a rake. But all young men tend to sow their wild oats and he does have redeeming attributes. He is intelligent, shrewd, resourceful and will make an excellent duke and I now believe an excellent husband. I see the way he looks at you. He is very much in love. Your personalities complement each other very well."

He placed a kiss on her forehead as they entered the house.

Adam joined his parents for luncheon at the family home and his grin that stretched from ear to ear indicated he had good news. As did the happy tune he kept whistling. His parents kept glancing at one another and back to him waiting for him to share what had made him so happy. Adam, feeling amused, stayed silent, knowing it was driving his mother crazy. His mother finally caved and, with little decorum, stood up and yelled across the dining table, knocking over her crystal flute of wine in the process.

"Damnation, Adam! Spit it out!" Adam laughed at his mother's exclamation, his emerald eyes flashing with merriment.

"Well, your grace, it appears I am a dutiful son indeed. You will be pleased to hear that you will no longer be parent to just I but my future bride, the Lady Charlotte Fitzroy. You will finally have a daughter and not just any but the one you had chosen."

All proprietary was lost as she lunged out of her chair to embrace Adam, while shouting, "I knew it over and over again!"

Amused at his wife's behaviour but pondering on Adam's words, his father asked his son,

"I know your mother made her intentions clear for you, but is this what you want, son? You have always thought of marriage as hell on earth."

Adam sobered, quickly turning serious.

"Yes, father. In all honesty, I can truly say I want to marry Charlotte. She is extraordinary. Her beauty, her brains, her spirit, I will be happy for all my days. And in truth, I am glad our duchess is so pushy." He winked at his mother, and she swatted him on the arm in return.

"We can announce the betrothal at our annual Portsmouth Garden Party. What a splash this news will make!"

"That is ages away," Adam moaned. "I was hoping to be married as quickly as possible."

"Hush, dear. No good ever comes of rushing these things. It just raises suspicions for scandal so do not even think of a special licence! This will be a wedding for the ages," she proclaimed firmly, "so not a word to anyone."

His father shook his head at Adam, indicating his mother would not be deterred. With a sigh, he asked a different question.

"I want the Fitzroy's to spend time with us. I was thinking of asking them to the Hallend Manor to show them around the estate and town."

His mother nodded excitedly.

"Yes, we will invite them for an evening, no, two, and we can all get acquainted, but as old family friends not as a betrothal, if anyone asks. We don't want any attention drawn away from a big announcement," she said, as plans started to form in her mind.

Adam spent the next hour listening to his mother talk wedding plans and, with a lopsided smile, decided he did not mind one bit.

Emma, ever an early riser, was on her way out, her maid Nancy in tow, when she heard the butler announce Lady Adele for her stepmother. She was instantly suspicious and decided to halt her plan to leave, gesturing the butler to be silent as she and her maid Nancy hid outside the door to her stepmother's sitting room. What on earth was she doing calling to visit so early, she wondered. Eavesdropping was not noble or ladylike; however, since Adele was a viper who could not be trusted, it was fair. Emma cringed at the high-pitched greetings the women gave one another. "Sit, darling, sit," cooed her stepmother Louise, Countess of Moreland. "What fabulous biting gossip do you have today?"

"Before we get into that, darling, I have had the most wonderful idea," Adele's falsetto voice loud and clear.

"Recall you were saying how boring the season was, I thought to myself, why don't you host a weekend at your country estate? Ellesmere, isn't it? And we can invite your step-daughter, of course, and those wallflower friends of hers. You have heard the rumours of Langdon dancing with Charlotte. If he is sniffing around her, we can include him and his friends Chester, Whitby and Drummond. You know how we enjoy being around handsome men." Without stopping for a reply, she continued, "I was also thinking the Viscount Sheffield is very handsome and that buffoon Percy at least is amusing."

Emma did not need to see her stepmother's face to know she was all for the idea, as she heard a high-pitched squeal and the sound of china clattering as a tea cup hit the saucer.

"That is a splendid idea! And Moreland is busy the upcoming weekends. I will not have to worry about him attending and can just enjoy myself. Now who else should we invite?"

The ladies started to expand the guest list, deciding on fifty guests. Emma shook with anger, hearing the way Louise dismissed her father, like he was a chore. Nancy gave Emma a sympathetic squeeze, knowing how much this bothered Emma.

It was known to all that the countess, who was only older than Emma by a few years and significantly younger than the earl, was a selfish woman who married for convenience not genuine affection. Emma's younger brother, Colin, was only four when her father remarried and had hoped for a mother figure, as she had died shortly after his birth, but it was Emma who he had come to see as his mother, as the countess had little regard for children. Now he was nine and at Eton and Emma missed him terribly but her charitable work at the orphanage kept her busy. And now she thought, as she signalled for her maid, that they could take their leave, she needed to send her note pre-warning her friends of Adele's machinations before they received her stepmother's invite. Devil only knows what agenda the viper had, probably trying to charm a new lord into her bed now the marquess was finished with her. If only I could also warn Lucas, she thought. She quickly brushed that thought aside, knowing it was silly to even think such a thing. *Anyway*, she thought, *if he attended, it means I will get to spend time with him as well.*

Adele left the Moreland residence feeling as a cat let free in a canary cage as she draped herself across the seat of her carriage. She took in her self-satisfied smirk in the mirror and laughed. She could always rely on Louise to go along with anything she requested! It still peeved her that Louise was a countess, but at least she had some usefulness. *Now the difficult part*, Adele thought, the smug feeling slowly abating. She needed to ensure that she got Adam and Charlotte in the same place to cause a rift, sending a note for a lovers' meeting was one thing but to foresee any obstacles was another. She decided her maid, who was loyal to her without a fault, would need to be engaged to assist in delivering the notes and help her keep an eye on Sheffield, so he did not screw anything up. Adele's smug feelings returned. *All will go to plan,* she told herself, *and once Adam sees Charlotte wrapped in the arms of another, he will understand what it is to feel rejected. And I will be there to console him, back in his bed where I belong. He really is the most magnificent love.* She sighed. *Oh, to watch that massive ego of his be shot to pieces,* she thought maliciously.

Chapter Thirteen

Washed up from her gardening, Charlotte took to the library with the intention of curling up with a good book; however, Aunt Anne bustled in the room waving paper.

"Charlotte, you have received two invitations and two notes."

Handing them to her, Aunt Anne sat down opposite with an expectant stare. Charlotte blushed, wondering if a note was from Adam, and looked up at her Aunt, wishing for some privacy. Aunt Anne began to laugh.

"I am just curious for the invitations, my dear, not your love notes," she said with a wink. Charlotte blushed and laughed.

"Oh, hush you or I will never cease blushing!" She had not been able to stop her wayward thoughts of Adam. *I am such a ninny*, she told herself, smiling.

Setting the notes aside, she opened the first invitation, which bore the Moreland insignia and was addressed to her with a small note for her father. She quickly skimmed the contents before reading out aloud.

The Countess of Moreland invites you to an intimate gathering at the Ellesmere Estate on Friday 13th March and Saturday 14th March.

Charlotte, as a friend of Emma's, will not require a chaperone. I will task myself with that duty.

Charlotte and Aunt Anne stared at each other as they both let out an unladylike snort.

"Nil chaperones, more like she just wants to surround herself with people closer to her own age." Charlotte agreed. The countess was a vain woman.

"I will take Macy, of course. She always watches out for me. Do you think father will mind?"

"No, he trusts you, plus we would not want to insult the countess with my presence," Aunt Anne said with an eye roll.

Giggling at her aunt, she mused out loud about who else would be invited.

"Wondering if a certain marquess is invited?" asked Aunt Anne with raised eyebrows, which made Charlotte blush again and she opened the next invitation.

"Moving along, dear Aunt, this second one is from the Duchess of Portsmouth, who invites you, father and myself to Hallend for the weekend to spend time getting acquainted with one another."

"Who has invited us where, Charlotte?" her father asked, as he joined them in the library. Charlotte quickly went over the invites, and he agreed for Charlotte to respond in the affirmative for them both.

Kentwell could see how happy Charlotte was and it warmed his heart. *So much like her mother, vibrant and happy,* he remembered with a touch of sadness. He was pleased her season was going so well on her own terms. Her antics amused him. She was just as he raised her with a strong mind of her own. He was also secretly pleased he would not have to endure gentleman after gentleman seeking her hand. *Bunch of coxcombs,* he thought. Langdon, despite his poor reputation, had turned out to be not such a poor choice as a future son-in-law. And he knew the Portsmouths would dote on her as well. He still felt remorseful at cutting Lydia out all those years ago. Just as he went to sit and make himself comfortable, Anne stood up.

"Let us give Charlotte some privacy to finish her correspondence. Off we go, old man." Shaking his head in good humour, he followed her out of the library. Charlotte settled back and opened the first note, which was from Adam. Reading his words made her heart beat faster as awareness ran through her.

I look forward to our time at Hallend and showing you the estate, especially if I can get you all to myself again. I find myself missing you when we are apart and long for the day we can start and finish each day together. I head to Hallend tomorrow and will see you in two days' time. Your ardent admirer, Adam.

Sighing happily, she clutched the note to her chest. How wonderful to be wanted so. *How did I ever think him to be such an unscrupulous fellow?* She opened the next note from Emma and the contents brought a frown to her forehead.

Charlotte, my dear friend, you would have received an invite from my stepmother. I want to give fair warning that the Lady Adele will be in attendance and strangely enough it was her suggestion my stepmother host the event and invite us and Langdon and his friends. It may mean nothing, but I wanted to pre-warn you that she will be there, especially after her behaviour last time. However, I am pleased to spend time with my wonderful friends and Ellesmere is a beautiful estate. Your dear friend, Emma.

Charlotte pondered over this strange information as she completed her replies to be sent in the morning. She kept her reply to Adam brief but sweet in case it missed him before he left and someone else read it. She relaxed into her chair and let her mind wander as she flipped through the pages of her book. She may not have entered society and been everyone's example of perfect, but she had made three genuine and wonderful friends. And the men may only see her outside appearance and wealth and care little for who she was on the inside but that did not matter either now that she had Adam. He liked her just the way she was.

Charlotte was reading a book of sonnets as she travelled to Hallend Manor. The Kentwell carriage ensured every possible comfort for the 4-hour trip. Spacious, the seats were wide and long, cushioned and trimmed with soft velvet. Her father was unable to come, being called away to his own estate at the last minute, so it was just her, Aunt Anne, and Macy in the carriage. The other two ladies were content with their embroidery. Macy had her tongue sticking out, biting it in concentration. Charlotte, however, was feeling restless and unable to focus on her book. She had brought Cleo along and, at the next stop, she decided she would ride her the rest of the way. Despite her aunt's protests, she had worn riding breeches and tailcoat, not the formal one she had made but more what the young men wore. Actually, it was what the men wore. *And yes, while she looked manly, it was more comfortable and who would recognise her out here? Furthermore, Hallend would need to adjust to her unusual ways.* She was eager to see Adam, missing him more than she felt would ever be possible the last few days.

It was a shame, she thought regretfully, *that this weekend they would be chaperoned at every turn.* She was feeling eager to explore the newfound passion he had awoken in her. She found it very curious that it was only he who made her feel this way, no other man she had danced with or who drew closer than was seemly ever sent her pulse racing. Just conversing with him and being in his very presence gave her satisfaction. This must be what love is, that special connection you only ever have with a single person. Looking back to her aunt and Macy, still absorbed in their work, she let out a discontented sigh resigning herself to the tedium. But as luck would have it, the coachman called for the final stop before they reached the estate. With an unladylike leap, she hurled herself out of the carriage, legs flinging out easy and wide in her breeches.

"Bit eager are we, my lady?" asked Macy with a knowing grin, as Aunt Anne admonished her for her lack of grace.

After they refreshed themselves and had a short rest, they commenced the rest of the journey. Charlotte mounted Cleo, grateful for her comfortable riding gear and set off at a trot, making distance past the carriage.

Chapter Thirteen

The duke and duchess watched their son in amusement as he fussed with the servants like an old woman wanting everything to be perfect. The housekeeper, Mrs Jones a conservative and competent woman, looked a little put out by all his interference. And in fairness, Adam had never once involved himself in the running of the house. Whenever the duke and duchess were in residence, they always took a guest room, leaving Adam the master bedroom despite his protests. The duchess now pondered over the proprietary of putting Charlotte in the adjoining room seeing as they were not yet married. The duke suggested that Kentwell may not be impressed with the close proximity, and Charlotte was instead placed in the same wing as the master bedroom but at the end of the hall and Aunt Anne in another room close by. Adam had made the servants move furniture and decor from the room adjoined to his to the one assigned to Charlotte, wanting her to be ensconced in all the luxury he had to offer. A servant rushed over and announced a carriage was making its way to the gates and Adam and his parents made their way outside.

Charlotte, still astride Cleo, made her way ahead of the carriage and took in her surroundings. Every sight she saw was beautiful. The gardens and landscaping were immaculate. English Oaks stood tall, lush green hedges lined the pathways and an assortment of vibrant colours filled the flower beds. A large sandstone water fountain, topped with an angel with wings, was pouring water in a gentle stream, the sound melodious to her ears. As she approached the front of the estate, she could see Adam and his parents and a row of servants awaiting her arrival at the front door at the bottom of the stairs. When she got closer, she saw their smiling faces but, when she looked over to the servants, she saw some expressions of shock as they took in her attire. Sighing, she felt some self-doubt about her impulsive clothing choice and began to fret Adam and his parents would be embarrassed.

Adam was thinking the exact opposite as he rushed over to assist her dismount before anyone else could. She looked marvellous in her riding wear, which was similar to his own, and what he imagined would be more comfortable. He appreciated her fine figure just the same as when he had first seen her in her formal riding gear. She saw the joy on his face and her self-doubt washed away. He gave her a small bow as he took her hand in his and pressed his lips to her knuckles, not once but twice!

"My lady, how pleased I am that you are finally here."

Blushing, she turned to greet his parents, as Adam greeted Aunt Anne.

"Your Grace, Duchess, thank you for the invitation," she responded with a curtsey. They were both smiling warmly at her, and the Duchess reached out and hugged her, exclaiming how pleased they were she had arrived.

Adam, eager to get Charlotte inside and refreshed so they could go exploring the estate, led her over to his staff.

"Let me introduce our guests, Lady Charlotte Fitzroy, the Duke of Kentwell's daughter, and her aunt, Lady Anne Fitzroy."

The servants curtsied, the shock worn off now they had seen how their Lord saw no issue with his lady's attire; however, Mrs Jones still appeared scandalised. Adam directed Macy to Mrs Jones, who guided her to their guest's rooms and to assist in putting their things away. Charlotte insisted she did not need any refreshment or rest and was eager to go on a tour. Aunt Anne, on the other hand, stated she did need rest and conferred with the duchess. As the estate was so busy, they agreed no escort was required. Not believing their luck at getting to spend time alone together, Adam and Charlotte avoided looking at each other in case their eagerness was mirrored as they went to mount their horses. They laughed as Argo snorted and sniffed at Cleo, who threw her head back at him with disregard.

Adam started with a tour of the grounds, gardens, the orchard and hot houses for flowers and fruits. He left the most impressive for last, the stables. He showed her his plans for the breeding program and the upgrades he had made, introducing her to some of the horses. He grinned as he watched her explore every nook and cranny and greet each horse warmly. The stable smelt of expensive horse and fresh hay, a smell they both appreciated.

"Maybe we should breed Argo and Cleo like you suggested. They would surely make an impressive foal and, unlike us, they do not have to be married to begin procreating."

She looked around to see if anyone had heard and gave him a smack on the arm.

"My Cleo is a lady and will need more attention than the silly snorts Argo has thrown her way! And as for you, maybe I will have to insist we prolong our betrothal so you can get your lust under control."

Her teasing tone took away the tartness of her remark. Unable to resist, he pulled her into his arms and found her lips with his own. Charlotte instantly melted against him, his kiss soft but insistent, their hearts beating fast against one another.

"I don't think there is anything possible that will curb the lust I have for you. It is unparalleled," Adam said softly, with all seriousness, before kissing her again, more deeply this time. He moved his hands down her body, sliding them under the sweep of her breasts, the curve of her waist and her rounded hips before cupping her bottom and pulling her close against him. Charlotte could feel his arousal through his breeches, igniting her own. As they came up for air, she could not resist another tart reply.

"Unparalleled? After all your years of debauchery, I suppose I should feel flattered?" Adam's only reply was a groan before he placed some separation between them.

"I curse my mother's insistence we keep this quiet and your father's agreement. The next weeks will be torture!" he grumbled. Their parents had met yesterday without them and decided as such, and her father had agreed to await announcing the betrothal and for a wedding at the end of the season.

"I know. I was also looking forward to a quick wedding, but our parents are right. As much as I do not care for the ton, I wouldn't want our married life to be surrounded by rumours like you were marrying me for some scandalous reason. Like procreation as you called it," she said with a blush. Her blushes squeezed his heart. They were so precious, since she was rarely anything but confident. The blushes were a sign she was affected by him. He could not help but drop a kiss to the tip of her nose and make a final quip.

"Let us continue to see some of the farms and tenants before I throw any caution to the wind and have my way with you in the hay."

This earned him another slap on the arm, and they remounted their horses.

Hallend was an extremely large estate, with its own town, Hallender, and numerous farms, but Adam only took her to the two closest, as they day was passing on. The Eaton family grew wheat and barley and the Jensens raised pigs. It was obvious that, though working class, the families were healthy, well-fed, and looked after by Adam. He was even on a first-name basis with the adults and children. He left her with the women while he went to talk with the men and she saw the women take in her clothes, Mrs Jensen eying her curiously.

"You ain't like no lady I've seen but neither is our Lord like others we hear of. Not that we've met many, mind ya. But aye, you will make a fine couple." She nodded with certainty. Her toddler Lucy tottered over and gave Charlotte a gummy smile as she hoisted herself up on to her lap.

Charlotte appreciating the candour and acceptance, thanked Mrs Jensen as she settled Lucy on her lap.

"Lucy Jensen! Do not haul yaself all over the lady's fine dress." Mrs Jensen scolded. Charlotte laughed with good humour.

"Do not fret, I love children and wee Lucy is just precious," she stated with genuine warmth as she smiled back at the little girl.

"Milord is very good with the young uns always has a smile or time for quick play when he comes past." Mrs Jensen said nodding approvingly.

Mrs Eaton, now the ice was broken, offered her opinion as they watched the men talk and laugh close by as the children ran around.

"He is a fine young man our Lord. He helps out at

harvest and contributes to the wages of others who help tend the crops every day. We are beholden to him, we are," she said, nodding humbly herself. Thanking Mrs Eaton for her kind words, Charlotte thought *how lucky am I to be marrying such a good-hearted man.*

Chapter Fourteen

After they got back to the estate, Charlotte and Adam retired, washed and changed for dinner. The duchess had ordered a simple but elegant dinner where they could speak comfortably and get to know one another. Lady Helen, a friend of the duchess, had joined them and had become fast friends with Aunt Anne while Charlotte was out with Adam. Between the six of them, there was much merriment over dinner. Once they had finished, they moved to the parlour and the sounds of Bach floated through the room. Lady Helen played the pianoforte and was highly skilled. As they listened, Charlotte, who was seated on a chaise with the duchess, quietly asked a question she had had in the back of her mind all day. She was annoyed with herself for caring about perception but it made her realise how important this relationship was, especially as her future mother-in-law.

"I hope I did not cause any embarrassment with how I turned up today, your grace, in my attire," she mumbled contritely.

The duchess smiled warmly, hearing her tone. She grabbed Charlotte's hand and gave it a squeeze.

"Of course not. Do not fret. Is it what society expects, no? But Adam does not care and nor do I. We are on our own estate. It isn't like you showed up at Almack's dressed this way."

Charlotte and the duchess both laughed at the scenario, imaging the horrified looks on the patronesses' faces.

"Your mother was not one for convention either. She hated wearing a dress while riding, and I daresay, if she had thought of what you had, it would have been a trend long beforehand. Adam told me about your riding habit. I have also heard it from some of the ladies while out and, rest assured, we will start to see more ladies dressed that way."

She had a sense of understanding now with the comparison to her mother.

"I see now why my father is so indulgent of me. When it was time to learn embroidery, I asked to learn archery. When he realised I was never going to be able to paint a pretty picture, he taught me billiards," she said, feeling some emotion well within her.

"Another thing your mother enjoyed. She confessed that your father taught her so well, she had to pretend to let him win at times."

Winking conspiratorially, Charlotte pronounced, "So do I!" making the duchess laugh heartily. Feeling at ease and comforted by the comparison to her mother, they turned back to the music.

Adam watched this exchange as he played cards with his father and was happy that his mother and Charlotte had a close relationship. Sighing with contentment as he shuffled the deck of cards to play another round of whist, he turned to his father.

"How swell this is all turning out. I never wanted marriage, but now I am in this position, after finding the perfect woman, I could not be gladder. Everything is just perfect."

The duke, happy for his son, agreed with him. But could not help a jibe.

"I told you one day you would change your mind. And this is why I tell you, my son, that your father is always right."

Looking at the mischievous twinkle in his father's eye, Adam could not help but chuckle. "Aye, you are. I look forward to saying the same to my own sons one day."

He looked back over to catch sight of her again and caught her eye. She signalled him over.

"What say you to a game of billiards?" she asked with an impish smile. Seeing his mother was also amused, he went along with them.

"You two are up to something but, of course, let us play. But I warn you, I play to win."

This caused peals of laughter between the two.

"I predict a long, happy marriage with no dull moments between you two," grinned his father.

Three neck-to-neck games later, with Charlotte winning two out of three, his father's words made sense. Adam made Charlotte swear not to tell his friends and she could beat him whenever she liked.

"All jests aside, you make me proud, sweetheart. In fact, I am going to make you verse my friends and show them up as well," he said, refraining from kissing her laughing mouth in front of their audience.

As the night wound up, she found herself hit with exhaustion, yawning loudly and not remembering to cover her mouth. Aunt Anne smiled and shook her head. Adam announced tomorrow's plans: the ladies would spend the morning doing whatever they pleased and, after luncheon, he would take Charlotte on a surprise outing. In the evening, a neighbouring estate had invited them to a small affair. Charlotte, satisfied with those plans, took herself off to bed, prepared to get a solid sleep to enjoy the following day. She was curious for her surprise. The guest room was decorated beautifully. Her feet stepped onto a plush, mahogany Aubusson rug, and elegant, cherry oak furniture filled the spacious room. Running her fingers across the fine craftsmanship, a purple hue caught her eye. A bunch of those purple roses were sitting on the bed, propped against her pillow with a note attached. Inhaling the beautiful fragrance, she read the note.

Sweet dreams, my darling. I am so happy that I get to call you mine. I count down the days till I can call you wife. Adam.

The four ladies enjoyed a lovely breakfast in the garden the next morning before heading out to Hallender, where the Duchess could show Aunt Anne, Lady Helen, and her around. The town was quaint and charming and, despite the age gap between the women and her, Charlotte truly enjoyed their company, especially when the Duchess made references to her mother. For so long, all she had was her childhood memories and ones from her father and Aunt. Knowing what her mother was like at a similar age to Charlotte now and before her marriage made her see just how much they had in common. Before they headed back for the midday meal, she pulled her future mother-in-law aside, gave her a warm hug and simply said, "Thank you".

"You are welcome, my dear. I see you as a daughter and you are by far the best decision my son has ever made."

Adam turned up halfway through lunch and quickly ate his meal, not wanting to waste any minute of his time with Charlotte. As she was still in her morning dress, he bid her to quickly change into her clothes from yesterday, as they would be more suited to his plans. She located the pants easily but had a maid fetch her one of Adam's shirts. Pulling it over her body gave her a tiny thrill. Adam grabbed her hand and got her jogging with him across the grounds, making them feel like children. They were breathless with laughter as he brought them to a stop. He had noticed she wore one of his shirts and he found it highly erotic. Guiding her through a copse of trees, they emerged on the other side where there was stream. She saw two fishing rods sticking out of the dirt and two buckets, and she suddenly knew what his surprise was. Squealing with joy, she grabbed his face in her hands and kissed him.

"You really are the most wonderful man and I still have yet to thank you for my roses," she said, giving him another kiss. He was thrilled and, not only because she was happy with his surprise, but also because this was the first time she had initiated any affection. He kissed her back, reigning in his own passion, as he truly did not know how much longer he would be able to control himself before he threw any chivalry away and made love to her here and now. Looking into her beautiful eyes, all dreamy and soft, he felt tempted to tell her he loved her but could not get the words to form in his mouth. *It's too soon*, he told himself. *I don't even know what love is.* Though he was certain this was what he felt for her, he was cowardly even to admit it to himself.

Spinning her around instead, he settled her along the grassy bank of the stream. The clean smell of the water and fresh scent of grass and dirt assaulted their senses and they breathed in deeply. They smiled at each other in understanding of their shared appreciation for nature.

"To make things interesting, I thought we would swap our bait preferences. I will use the worms and you will use the squid and we will see who catches the most fish," he said, giving her a charming wink.

"Who would have thought a childhood quarrel would bring about such a wonderful time together as adults?" she said, kicking off her shoes and baiting her hook.

"I wish we had more memories together. I can only remember a few clearly and you were quite bossy and argumentative, my little shrew," he teased affectionately, "but this is my most vivid memory, when a little mite of a girl tried to tell me how to fish!"

The sun was shining on his face highlighting his golden hair and reflecting off his emerald eyes, which were twinkling with devilish merriment. Nostalgic with the childhood memory they shared, Charlotte nodded, emotion catching in her throat, and she busied herself with reeling her line into the water. They fell into companionable silence as they fished and enjoyed each other's company and, before long, Charlotte had caught two trout and Adam had caught two more.

Charlotte asked Adam to tell her about his friends when

they stopped for refreshment. Adam was prepared with a basket of food he had left on a sturdy branch to keep the ants at bay. Before going into individual detail, he explained they went to Eton together and were all in the same year and, for whatever reason, they had just clicked.

"We were friends with the other boys, but it was just our group we really trusted and relied on. Lucas was only a teen when his father passed, and the Earldom fell to him. His mother is a tyrant and he does his best to keep her happy. Anthony inherited his viscount title only last year when his father passed and has been a bit harried since, taking over the responsibility, but he does not talk much about it. Jeremy has held the barony for a few years and is obscenely wealthy. He has made some good investments, and we all take advice from him, as he is good with numbers. He has Scottish roots but does not like to talk about his long family history." She was pleased with his detailed response and that he held nothing back.

"And how did you all become a band of rogues?" she teased.

"I am not at liberty to divulge; we have a pact that what happened between any open thighs, ah I mean, behind closed doors just stays between us. But what I can say, we are all good looking, young, rich, titled men." Rolling her eyes, she laid back on the grass.

"What about your group of friends, bluestockings as you say. How did that come about? And I have to say, I am glad you have bluestocking friends and not the other empty-headed chits floating around this season."

Laughing at his comment and biting back a retort about Portia, she explained how it had come to be.

"At my coming out ball, I saw them against the wall, not acting missish or seeking attention and knew they would be my type of friends. We have so much in common: we like to read, ride, discuss politics, but they care naught if I act a little less ladylike than others. I am still learning about them, but Emma is a dutiful daughter, shrew and warm. Her stepmother is a nightmare. Eleanor lives with her uncle, who became her guardian after she was orphaned, and they are close. Harriet does not talk much about her family, and I do not like to pry."

Pausing, she suddenly exclaimed.

"The Moreland weekend in the country! Are you going to attend? I forgot all about it!" Laughing, Adam said, "I wanted to ask you but forgot also. I have been so distracted with enjoying the now, but I responded yes as I knew you would go for Emma. If you do not go, I will send my apologies. You are my only incentive."

It occurred to her that she had not informed Adam of Emma's suspicions. Just as she was about to broach the topic, she saw him throw his head back to the sky and sniff the air. She followed his line of sight and saw smoke tinged with red. Adam jumped, grabbed her hand and quickly led her back, stating he was going to make haste to the stables.

"I am going to ride in that direction of the fire. You go inside and inform my father just in case they have not been alerted. Stay here. It may not be safe."

Giving her a fast kiss, he rode off bareback on Argo, only placing his reins. Charlotte went inside, running for the duke, who she almost bowled over as he came around the corner. She told him what was going on. Charlotte went to sit with the ladies and, after 30 minutes, announced she could not stand the waiting and went to saddle Cleo to ride and check Adam was unharmed. He might be furious she had not listened, but his wrath would be worth it for her own peace of mind.

When Adam reached the site of the fire, he found it was the Jensen's homestead burning. He saw there were already people gathered, who were starting to make a water bucket line. Adam quickly joined in and, not long after, saw his father had also joined the line. It was a long and slow process, and he knew it would take time to make a dent in the flames.

"Where is Lucy," wailed Mrs Jensen her hands wrung in distress.

"I thought you had her," cried out her husband, distraught emotion evident on his face.

The people gathered started to shout out, "Lucy, Lucy," and shortly after one of the men closer to the homestead yelled out, "I think I hear something."

Adam did not even think before he ran in after telling the others to stay back. He entered the fiery homestead, the thick black smoke stifling as he lifted his shirt to cover his mouth, looking to see where Lucy had gone. He heard her cries coming from a room on his left and quickly followed the sound but, as he made his way into the room, a smouldering, wooden beam dropped off the ceiling onto his arm, burning his flesh. Cursing at the stinging sensation, he ignored the pain and saw Lucy huddled under the bed, the orange flames licking at the walls. Reaching her quickly and hauling her up in his arms, he shielded her with his body and quickly made his exit.

Charlotte had arrived on the scene the moment Adam had run into the inferno. If she had not been sitting on Cleo, her body would have collapsed to the ground. The duke saw her and quickly got her down off the horse. He looked just as stricken as she did. She was ready to chase after Adam, but his father would not let her go. It seemed so much longer than the few minutes they waited but, before they could fall apart any further, Adam emerged from the flames with the little girl in his arms. They raced over to him, as did the Jensen's. The relieved and sobbing family thanked Adam profusely as Mrs Jensen grabbed a weeping Lucy into her arms. Thankfully, the doctor had arrived as well. Adam was too exhausted to even berate Charlotte and just held her as the doctor tended to his arm. His father alternated between scolding his recklessness and praising his bravery.

The combined efforts of the water line started to take effect and the fire was slowly put out. The doctor confirmed both Adam and Lucy had slight smoke inhalation and the burn on Adam's arm would heal. It would be painful and tender for a week or so, so he gave him some salve.

Once they arrived back home, there were tears and fussing all round from the women.

"Adam did what," yelled the duchess in alarm.

"Calm yourself love, he is alright and he is a hero," the duke said comfortingly.

"You really care for your tenants, don't you, Adam," nodded Aunt Anne with understanding. "Charlotte's father is exactly the same."

"The Jensen's are good people, they all are. Such a terrible tragedy but at least no lives were lost," said Adam with gruff feeling.

Everyone was feeling emotionally exhausted and, after having a quick repast, the duke suggested they all turn in. Adam and Charlotte, with not a moment to spare alone, shared a goodnight with the rest of the group and made their way back to their separate rooms.

Chapter Fifteen

Charlotte bathed and changed into her nightgown. She was wearing a matching robe of soft, pale-pink silk and was pacing the length of her room. She could not sleep or relax and had this whirling sensation churning in her belly. She did not want to be alone; she wanted to be with Adam! What happened tonight was a reminder of how short life can be, how tragic accidents can occur in the blink of an eye, exactly what had happened with her own mother. Yes, Adam was going to be fine, but the fear that had clenched her heart seeing him go into that burning home and not knowing if he would come out was a feeling so horrible, one she had never known and wished to never know again. Adam's room was only at the end of the hall; he was so close and yet so far.

Adam had changed for bed. He was just in his pants after finishing his bath, keeping his burn dry. He was sitting on a chair, sipping his whiskey, the events of the day washing over him as the adrenaline slowly left his body. Some might think he was foolish or reckless, as he was so often likened as, the only heir to a dukedom, running into an inferno. Shaking his head, he had no regrets. He was not any worse for wear, his arm stung like hell, but it was worth knowing the child was safe. What he really wished for now was to be alone with Charlotte, appreciating all life had to offer. The temptation, knowing she was close by, was frustrating him to no end. A knock on the door broke through his wistful thoughts. *Probably mother or father checking up on me*, he thought wryly. They had fussed over him well enough tonight like he was a little babe. Not answering verbally, he just opened the door and, when he saw who was on the other side, all his senses left him. *Christ*. He was in trouble.

Charlotte had waited for Adam to open the door, not knowing what she was even going to say and paranoid someone may come down the hall at any moment. When she had heard no reply, she assumed he may be asleep and, disappointed, started to turn away, until she heard the door open. Spinning around, her breath came out in a whoosh. Adam stood in the doorway, shirtless, his chest muscular and tanned, his pants sitting low on his slim hips. His golden hair was damp at the ends and curled up. She was reminded of those statues of Greek gods she saw in books; he truly was a magnificent piece of art. The tantalising scent of sandalwood lingered in the air from his bath. Adam was also staring, wondering how she could look so innocent but sexually enticing in her sweet pink nightgown and robe. A full minute would have passed before Adam came to his senses and pulled her into the room, shutting the door behind her.

"What's wrong, sweetheart?" he asked. "I was thinking about you and here you are. I feel as if I conjured you out of the air."

"I was thinking about you as well. I could not sleep. I

wanted to see how you were feeling and hold you, be close to you and ..."

Her voice became choked up and she could not get the rest of the words out. Pulling her into his arms, he hushed her, running his hands down her arms and her back, trying to soothe her. It was such a nice feeling, her caring for him this way. *I doubt any woman has ever held such genuine affection for me the way she does*, he thought. He bent his head into her soft hair, inhaling her scent of roses and femininity. *Christ*. She aroused him.

"I can assure you I am well. My arm stings and the coughing has eased. I can thank the good old Scottish whiskey for that," he grinned, trying to make light of the situation. Charlotte tilted her head up so their eyes met. The intimacy of the moment was not lost to them: half-dressed and alone. Charlotte could not help but say the following words out loud and Adam would be a liar if he said these were not words he desperately wanted to hear from her lips. She took a deep steadying breath, "I don't want to sleep alone. I want to stay with you. I know this isn't proper and you might say no, but I want to know you now, as a woman knows a man, as a wife knows a husband. Today made me realise how precarious life can be. Make love to me, Adam."

Adam stood frozen for a moment, filled with indecision, despite wanting the exact same thing. One part of his mind urged him to laugh that she thought he needed convincing. The other, some responsible part he was not accustomed to hearing in his mind, reminded him this was not proper. But staring into her eyes, her lush body pressed against him in an amorous embrace, he was unable to turn her away. Right or wrong was no longer a factor. They were to be married and, in all fairness to them, they would not be the first or last couple who had anticipated their wedding night. Rather than reply to what she declared, he lowered his head, their breath mingling for a moment before he took her lips. When he felt his measured kisses being returned by her own insistent kisses, his turned fierce. They clung to each other, desperately wanting no space between them in their passionate embrace, though she took care not to touch his injured arm. The heat emanating from their bodies made him feel he was caught in another inferno.

Charlotte was awash with sensation, his tongue was sweeping her mouth and tangling erotically with her own. He tasted of whiskey and pure masculinity. She wanted to devour his kisses, feeling almost greedy, as she took all that he had to offer. She felt his hands sweeping her shoulders and down her sides, no longer in comfort but in frenzied need. Charlotte heard him growl as he moved his kisses along her jawline and down her neck, ravishing the sensitive skin. Charlotte suddenly gasped out loud with pleasure as his hands pressed her bottom into his groin, rubbing his hardness against her own throbbing core.

Adam felt his self-control spiralling as the blood pounded at his temples. He knew Charlotte's was as well, which brought him back down to earth and cooled his ardour. Remembering she was innocent, he needed to go slow, despite her fiery, ardent response. He slowed his kisses, taking her mouth again, and started to walk backwards to the bed, halting at the edge. He looked at her face, her eyes closed and lips swollen and red from his kisses. Charlotte's eyes fluttered open, and stared back into Adam's, hooded with a sultriness that matched his own urgency.

"Are you sure this is what you want, Charlotte?"

His voice was harsh from breathing heavily. Her own voice was husky and one she did not recognise.

"Yes, I want you. I want you more than I want to take my next breath," she replied, her own breath coming out in pants.

Adam knew there was no turning back now, and he sat on the bed, positioning Charlotte to stand between his knees.

He reached up to her shoulders and pulled her robe down her arms, the soft silk sliding sensuously across her skin as it fell to the floor. She was filled with too much anticipation to feel shy as her nightgown fell next and puddled at her ankles. She stood naked in front of him. He was in awe at how smooth and curvaceous her body was; he had never seen such perfection. The brief look he had had when they had last been alone was nothing compared to what was before him now. He committed every detail to his memory. Her breasts were large, high, and firm. Her nipples hard, inviting and that dusty pink rose he found so tempting. Her waist was small and flared out to wide hips, legs curvy and lean. He reached his hands behind to cup her derrière, caressing the plump roundness. It was as if he had his very own Aphrodite rising from the foam. He traced his fingers up her spine and felt the erotic shiver he caused. Looking to her most tempting place, he sensed the arousal radiating from her and had to restrain himself from touching the soft chestnut curls and what lay beneath.

He suddenly realised his perusal may have made her uncomfortable but, when he looked at her face, all he saw was arousal.

"You are the most exquisite woman I have ever seen; I am so lucky to call you mine. You remind me of Aphrodite rising from the foam," he told her, placing a searing kiss just above her belly button. Her breath quickened at this intimate touch, and she bid him to stand, whispering, "now you". Flashing a grin, he stood, no qualms of shyness, and lowered his pants. Flicking them off to the side, he watched her curious eyes run over every inch of his hard body and twirling her finger for him to spin. Laughing at her boldness, he did as she bid. Charlotte was speechless, amazed that a man's body could be so beautiful. He was muscular all over his chest, his thighs, his buttocks. Of most interest to her roving eyes was his erection, standing proud and large, it was quite intimidating. Much larger than she remembered from when she had touched it that one time. Taking a breath, she refused to be missish, looked up into his eyes and told him exactly what she had been thinking as she ran her hands across his hair-roughened chest, feeling the shiver of arousal pass underneath her caress.

"I never knew the male body could be so beautiful. I think I am the lucky one," she said in a husky tone. Groaning with mindless need, he yanked her up to pull her against him and they both gasped at the bare skin contact, soft satin curves moulding against hard muscle.

Having their naked bodies pressed so intimately together almost undid Adam. No woman had ever made him feel this way, where he could lose control like an untried lad. He took her mouth in a searching kiss, as he picked her up and swung her gently down to the bed onto her back. He got in beside her and continued to plunder her sweet, warm mouth until they were breathless. He released her lips and started to press kisses along her neck, sucking the sensitive skin and causing a sharp intake of breath from her and a deep moan.

"Oh, Adam every part of my body is tingling in ecstasy."

Grinning against her satiny skin, he intended to make

her moan louder. He swirled his tongue in the hollow of her neck as his hands moved to her breasts, drawing circles around the flesh but avoiding her nipples. She started to move restlessly, her neck and breasts felt so sensitive. He was driving her mad with the teasing caresses. She wanted to tell him to touch her the way he had last time, her body urging him, as she felt them aching for his touch. He sensed her frustration and his lips widened against her skin. She felt the flicker of his tongue across one tight nipple and his fingers rolling the other. The incredible sensation it aroused went all the way down to her core and she could feel the wetness between her legs. He took her nipple in his mouth, sucking gently, but the more restless she became the harder and rougher he sucked. She began to moan and fisted her hands in his hair to hold him in place. Adam moved to the next breast, giving it the same attention, and he heard her pant with pleasure. He could sense her control snapping, and so was his own, but he needed to make her ready for him to ease any pain. He had never been with a virgin, and he wanted to make this memory beautiful, not painful.

Adam moved down from her breasts, tracing kisses along her stomach and around her belly button, dipping his tongue, and felt her stomach muscles clench. Daringly, he continued even lower. Charlotte was too caught up in how amazing he was making her feel that it was not until she felt him press his lips against the entrance to her body that she gave a little jump. Adam pressed his hand on her belly feeling the muscles tighten. He stroked it gently and hushed her. "Trust me," was all he said. And she did. The scent of her moist heat was driving him insane and when he spread her softly to lick the centre of her, he growled with desire. He was like a man starved. The taste of her intoxicated him and he used his mouth and tongue to drive her mad with desire. *This is so wicked*, she thought. A real lady would show some restraint but the feel of him against her very core was wonderful and she wanted more. Her body eagerly pushed against him as she raised her hips in wild abandon. Adam knew she was close to climax, and he inserted one finger into her wet warmth and then another, thrusting them in and out in a tantalising motion. It was not long before he felt her body tense and cry out in pleasure as the tremors of fulfilment rippled across her body and he knew she was ready for him.

He caressed her trembling body tenderly, as he made his way back up her body kissing every part he could.

"I am going to make you mine now, my love. It may hurt a little bit and I will stop if you want me to."

Nodding, she reached for him, grasping his face in her palms to look him deeply in his jewelled eyes that shimmered with all the passion she felt. "I trust you."

He read the trust in her eyes and trailed kisses across her face as he tried to steady the lust pounding through him, urging him to take her. Gently, he parted her thighs and positioned himself against her opening, rubbing himself along the wetness before slowly guiding himself in. She started to feel nervous. It did not feel bad, just a little uncomfortable. He felt so large. He was going slowly and gently despite the fierce look on his face. He had never fought for so much self-control as he did in that moment, wanting her to become accustomed to his size and how this felt. Uncertainty warred within him when he met her barrier. *Do I do it slowly or just push through?* Thinking it would be better to just get it over with, he whispered, "This may hurt. Hold on to me," and pushed. Charlotte felt a pinch and he was fully inside her. After a few moments, as he kissed and caressed her, she started to feel her lust return and wanted him to move. Adam had been watching her expression, while he pressed soft kisses against her face, and saw the moment the lustful look came back into her eyes.

"I feel so complete, Adam."

Satisfied she was all right, he surrendered to his tortured body. On his first thrust, her ecstatic moan was all he needed to continue. He thrust slowly in and out in a steady rhythm, trying to go slow.

But she was moving underneath him wildly, her hands grabbing his hips trying to pull him further inside her. He grabbed her legs and told her to wrap them around his waist. He slid deeper inside of her, causing them both to moan out loud. He was feeling so many emotions and he dropped his head to kiss her roughly. She loved this feeling, their bodies joined as one was so intimate. He kissed her with such abandon, like she drove him just as crazy as he was driving her. She squeezed his forearms, needing to anchor herself to the cyclone of intensity that swirled inside her. Adam began to thrust faster and deeper, and she could feel the sensations building again, her muscles starting to tense and tingle, her breathing started to come in short gasps. Adam had his face buried in her neck, willing her to climax so he could join her. Her core was clenching around him, and Adam felt the tenseness in her body. He glanced at her face and saw her expression as she climaxed for the second time. This caused his own climax, as he came apart inside her. In the height of their mutual climax, Adam could not hold back how he was feeling and, in between his heavy breathing, uttered, "I love you". Charlotte caught up in her own maelstrom of emotion and sexual ecstasy did not even hesitate to say the words she also could not stop thinking, "I love you, Adam."

Chapter Sixteen

Adam had collapsed on top of Charlotte, the force of their lovemaking sapping him of all his strength. Worried he might be crushing her, he shifted his weight and Charlotte wrapped her arms around his waist.

"I like how you feel on top of me," she sighed. She never knew the weight of a man's body could feel so satisfying. They laid that way for a while, still catching their breath before they shifted. He wrapped his arms around her from behind, and they were silent for a few minutes, absorbing the moment until he spoke.

"How do you feel?" he probed tentatively.

"In truth, I feel wonderful. I did not know so much pleasure could be found in the act," she said, feeling her face redden with a blush at her bold statement.

Adam could not help his cocky grin. He could not help but be proud to be the first and now only man to be lucky enough to be with her.

"There was not much pain then?"

"No, just a pinch and just for a second, then it felt

wonderful again," she said, peeking a look at him, serious all of a sudden.

"Adam, is it always like that? Like when you are with other women?" His cockiness faded and a serious look came over his face.

Turning her on her back, so he could stare into her eyes, he expressed the words that came straight from his heart.

"No. Never have I felt the way that I feel with you. I know my past leaves much to be desired, but I can truly say that what we shared is new to me as well. And I meant it, that I love you. You are mine," he said, his tone growing fierce with possession.

"And you are mine. Oh no, is your arm all right? I forgot!"

"It is fine. You did a very good job while lost in passion to not touch it. I was a little worried, you wild wench," he teased her.

She giggled, the situation now a little incredulous.

"Who would have thought I could get a rogue such as yourself to settle down?"

Laughing, he remembered his own friends had predicted she would.

"Only you, my beautiful shrew. Only you."

He held her tight in his arms, his heart full of contentment.

"We have a few more hours before we have to sneak you back. We could get some sleep, or I can show you some more of roguish ways."

Her answer was simply a blazing kiss.

Charlotte returned from Hallend a different woman, both in mind and body. She wished she could speak with her friends about her love-making experience but felt too shy to bring it up, knowing they all retained their innocence. She sighed, as she recalled how she would not even see Adam for days now. He had not come back to town, deciding to stay at Hallend to heal for a few days before helping the Jensen's rebuild their homestead. Adam hoped to be back before they headed off to the Moreland estate, but it appeared she would be waiting until then to see him. Scolding herself for maudlin feelings, she went to her basin to splash cold water on her face. Her friends would arrive soon for their weekly tea, and she wanted to fill them in on everything else that had happened. Dabbing at her face with a soft white cloth, she hoped the glow she could see reflected in the mirror would not be too obvious. A secretive smile grew as she remembered the thrill of being in his arms.

The group of four sat in Charlotte's rose garden and the sounds of birds chirping and bugs cheeping made a lovely background noise. She had arranged their tea to be set up outside so they could enjoy the nature and sunshine. Harriet had brought her embroidery to work on, Eleanor was venting about her cousin who kept dropping hints he wanted her uncle to marry her off, and Emma was cross with her stepmother who had been exceedingly annoying since announcing her party, bossing everybody in the household around.

"Charlotte has the right of it, getting married. At least

she will be the mistress of her own home," grumbled Emma. She had confided in her friends about the betrothal, swearing them to secrecy, though she knew that went unsaid.

"Yes, but she gets to marry a young, handsome man. My cousin keeps suggesting men old enough to be my father, some even my grandfather! And he then says I should consider myself lucky seeing as I do not have a title," Eleanor stated heatedly.

"He needs a swift kick to the bollocks, your cousin," Charlotte offered, disheartened to see her usually bubbly friend so forlorn.

"Do not stress, Eleanor. Your uncle would never permit it. He sees you as a daughter. And I am sure he even realises the kind of man his son has grown up to be." Harriet squeezed her hand, smiling warmly.

"Thank you, dear friends. Charlotte, I can still not believe the marquess risked his life that way. Such a brave man!" Eleanor exclaimed.

"It was terribly frightening and, though I wish he hadn't, I cannot fault the man for being such a selfless soul," she sighed, causing Emma to giggle.

"Oh, you are so in love. It is so sweet! You must be dying to see him again."

"On that topic, what are our travel plans to Ellesmere?" Harriet asked.

"You can come with me, Harriet," Eleanor suggested.

"And, Charlotte, you and Macy can come with me, as there is no way I will be travelling with Louise less I strangle her on the way," Emma said, grimacing dramatically.

Giggling at Emma's theatrics, their talk moved onto the

book of the month. Charlotte had requested they all read *Taming of the Shrew*.

"I will go first," she said. "The line that resonates with me most is, '*I see a woman may be made a fool. If she had not a spirit to resist,*' and I think that speaks for itself, does it not ladies?" She grinned at her laughing friends.

Adam returned one day before he was due to depart for the Moreland affair. Adam did not care for the countess, finding her flightiness irritating and was so thankful he had never bedded her. Shuddering at the awkwardness if she had been one of the notches on his bedpost, he thanked his lucky stars she wasn't. It was too late to visit Charlotte, so he made his way to White's. And as luck had it, Lucas, Anthony, and Jeremy were laughing over a bottle of whiskey. Joining his friends, he breathed in the familiar scent of cigar smoke and smooth malted spirits. Pouring himself a glass as they cheered, calling him a hero, he waved them off with a good-natured shrug.

"Here he is, scoundrel, card shark, and now hero who runs into infernos," Jeremy hooted.

"Shame you got yourself betrothed. Women love a good story and scar," teased Anthony. He had sent them notes before he left for Hallend, knowing he could trust them to say naught. He still checked and looked around but saw no one was listening. Thinking of their betrothal reminded Adam of their lustful night and a satisfied smile appeared.

Lucas groaned, "Tell me you didn't?"

Jeremy and Anthony quickly caught on to what Lucas alluded to and mirth twinkled in their eyes.

"I can't confirm nor deny anything. All I will say is I am a lucky man, my friends."

He took their teasing; he was a besotted fool and glad of it. They began discussing the visit to Ellesmere tomorrow and decided to take separate carriages in case they got called away.

"Or we need to escape! I'm still not certain who is on that guest list, but I better not see any senseless chit sneaking into my room," Lucas said with a shudder.

"I would be more worried about the mature ladies. I hear Adele will be there and the Countess Louise. She loves seeking out attention from anyone not her husband. Strange how she is Lady Emma's stepmother," Jeremy raised.

"Emma's stepmother?" Lucas shot up in surprise.

"Emma, is it?" teased Adam.

Lucas rolled his eyes and made a mental note to steer clear of the countess. Since they were making an early start, they wrapped up the evening, clapping each other on the backs as they went into the night.

The Moreland carriage transporting the Countess of Moreland and Lady Adele to Ellesmere, was filled with incessant chatter. *Does Louise ever stop?* Adele thought, fighting the urge to roll her eyes while she smiled and nodded. She wanted peace and quiet to consider her plan. How to get Charlotte alone with Sheffield and Adam to stumble across them? What note could she write without drawing too much suspicion that the notes were false? Louise's prattling broke into her plotting.

"...We will have an early dinner and play games.

Tomorrow I have arranged for the men to go hunting and we can do watercolours. For the evening, we will do a masked ball. I have brought along a trunk filled with masks!"

"Sounds fabulous, darling. I love a bit of mystery and not knowing who is under a mask. It's all a little bit naughty," Adele laughing wickedly.

"Oh yes. I plan on finding myself caught in a dark corner with a nameless gent. I deserve some fun."

Wholly agreeing with her, Adele settled back into the seat, satisfied tomorrow's evening events would provide a perfect setting, ripe with confusion.

Charlotte stared out the carriage window as they arrived. Ellesmere was tremendous. It swept across the grounds, and it was easy to see how it boasted seventy bedrooms. Emma had explained that no guest needed to share a room and Louisa had hired extra staff for the weekend to cater to everything. Emma was a tad put out with how outrageous Louisa was acting but had begrudgingly admitted an entertaining weekend had been planned. Charlotte was on tenterhooks, nervous and excited to see Adam. They pulled up the immaculately landscaped path to the French-style front doors of Ellesmere and saw Louise and Adele exiting the carriage ahead. Rolling their eyes at each other, they went over to greet them. Louise spied them and pounced immediately.

"Wonderful. You two can stay in the foyer and greet the guests. Mrs Strand knows what rooms everyone is assigned and just entertain those who don't wish to rest, will you? I have an early dinner planned and games planned for the evening. Ta ta."

Louise sauntered off. With a vicious smirk aimed at Charlotte, Adele followed suit.

Emma looked down at her dress.

"Lucky we were practical and wore pretty morning dresses to avoid getting changed again."

Emma wore a lemon-yellow gown that brought out the blue in her eyes. Charlotte was in a soft green, a colour that always sat well against her chestnut hair. Linking arms and laughing, they headed to the foyer to make themselves comfortable and wait for the guests to arrive.

They greeted Eleanor and Harriet first and a few other guests shortly followed. Eleanor who excelled on the pianoforte started to play a lively Mozart while the guests took refreshment. Lucas and Anthony arrived at the same time and Emma blushed profusely as Lucas kissed her hand a few seconds longer than necessary. The next two to arrive forced them to suppress eyerolls – Portia and Eliza. The new arrivals offered a chilly greeting and swept by as if she and Emma were servants. A few seconds later, they heard the shrill squeal of Portia espying Lucas and Anthony. So engrossed they were with their spying, they did not see Adam arrive. He took the opportunity to surprise Charlotte, placing his hands around her waist and spinning her around. It was her turn to squeal as she spun around to face his cheeky grin.

Emma covered a hand over her mouth to hide her laughing, as Charlotte swatted Adam to put her down. Charlotte told him his friends were taking refreshment in the drawing room. Adam quickly looked around to ensure no one was watching, except Emma, before stealing a quick kiss. Reprimanding him, she showed him to the room and made a quick exit as Portia pretty much threw herself at him. Clenching her teeth, she returned to greet the last of the guests. The very last to arrive was Viscount Sheffield. Charlotte felt a little guilty at his overly warm greeting, recalling his interest in her. He was bound to be disappointed when her betrothal was announced. Joining the others, she noted Adele had also joined the guests and everyone seemed to be enjoying the good music and conversation.

Adam and Adele's attention focused on the two people who had just entered the room. Adam's eyes narrowed, seeing Sheffield standing close to Charlotte, touching her shoulder. *He should not be so familiar with her,* he thought angrily. *Even I am not able to be familiar with her in this setting.*

Adele's gaze was bouncing between Adam's scowl and the object of his attention and gratification flowed through her as the seed for her plan was planted.

Louise had planned an early dinner and made the seating arrangements. So, of course, Emma, Charlotte, Eleanor, and Harriet found themselves at the end of the dining table. To Charlotte's right was James and her left Percy, or the drunken fool, as she had since dubbed him. Adam was at the other end of the table seated between Louise and Portia. Both were unhappy about the seating arrangements but, with the way Adam was glowering at her, she wondered if the distance was a good thing. *What does he expect, the jealous buffoon? That I ignore my dinner partners?* His own dinner partners were not ideal either as they both flirted and vied for his attention. Resolved to enjoy the evening, she decided she would not look at him for the rest of dinner.

Adam noticed Charlotte's ignorance of him during dinner and was a little hurt by her snub. *Can she not even spare a smile for her betrothed?* His attention was not focused on his surroundings, which kept provoking Portia and Louise to pull on his shirt sleeves, trying to gain his attention.

"We heard what happened, my lord. You truly are a hero," Portia said in a syrupy tone and with a flutter of her eyelashes.

"You will have to show me in private if you have a scar," whispered Louise seductively.

Stifling a groan, he looked at Jeremy's amused face across from him. He turned to Louise.

"It is just on my arm, nothing exciting, but, if scars interest you, my lady, I know the Baron has one on his chest and the Earl on his left buttock."

Lucas, who was on the other side of Louise, overheard Adam and made a choking noise as he attempted to swallow the bite of food in his mouth. Anthony, who was sitting beside Adele, was also facing unwanted attention. Whether she was just feeling lustful or trying to make Adam jealous, as Anthony assumed, her fingers kept grazing his thigh and were becoming a nuisance. Throwing back his whiskey in one gulp, he caught Adam's grin, who had seen what was going on and shook his head.

Dinner started to wind down and Louise announced the evening entertainment: playing parlour games – Charades, Consequences and Buffy Gruffy. Soon the room was filled with guests shouting and laughing, almost everyone was having a grand time. Adam was paired with Emma and Harriet during a round of a game and found he was enjoying himself in their company. They were humorous and witty, not silly, much like Charlotte. Glancing over, he saw her laughing with Jeremy and Eleanor and he was glad Sheffield was not hanging over her. Looking around, he was surprised to see Sheffield and Adele with their heads bent together whispering.

Nudging Anthony, he said, "You won't have to bar your door tonight, seems she found new prey."

Anthony spoke a prayer of thanks, "I will be passed out soon if I keep drinking, so I would not have remembered a thing anyway!"

Emma noticed Louise was also a bit worse for wear and beginning to slur her words.

She was whispering these same concerns in Eleanor's ear and Adam overheard.

"Let me, my lady." He cleared his throat and clapped his hands, gaining everyone's attention. "It is high time we call it a night, ladies and gents. We have another full day tomorrow, off to bed."

He grinned at Emma, and she thanked him profusely.

"Do not thank me, just pass this message on for me," and he whispered in Emma's ear.

Disappointed the night had ended and she had barely said two words to Adam, Charlotte darted upstairs. Emma knocked on her door shortly after to wish her goodnight and had a message.

"Adam wanted me to tell you how much he missed you today, and he wishes you good sleep."

Thanking her friend, she readied herself for bed knowing tomorrow would be a better day.

Chapter Seventeen

"It was not a better day," Charlotte grumbled to herself, as she stared out across the rolling green grass. *Today was awful!* Louise had set up easels for the ladies to paint a watercolour of Ellesmere. She was terrible at painting and wished she could have gone hunting with the gents. But she wanted to show everyone that she was a lady in preparation of her upcoming nuptials.

"I now sorely regret this choice," she mumbled under her breath, "And this is why my motto is to care for no one's opinion."

Sensing her melancholy mood, Harriet, who was the most creative, drew closer in support.

"You look so miserable."

"I am miserable. Look at the atrocity in front of me."

They stared at her painting.

"It is not that bad; I can see you have painted the grass a nice shade of green."

Harriet spoke with genuine sincerity, despite the greenish-brownish blob. Giggling at Harriet's attempt to make her feel better, she hugged her friend.

"You have not a mean bone in your body."

Harriet turned to focus back on her own painting, which of course looked like a masterpiece ready to be framed. She turned to her own painting but had nil enthusiasm and went over to Emma and Eleanor.

"What are you two wearing tonight?"

Happily discussing their gowns for the evening, they did not notice someone approach Charlotte's easel, until mocking laughter broke into their conversation as Emma finished describing her dress.

"Who on earth painted this monstrosity?" came the tart voice of Adele. *Of course*, thought Charlotte, as she turned around, *Of course it's her*.

"It does not look like a lady even touched it, but some uncultured peasant who has never held a paintbrush!"

She felt her face turn bright red, a combination of anger and embarrassment. Drawing herself up to her full height, she turned and faced her nemesis.

"It is mine. Thank you for the feedback, insulting as it was."

She hoped her approach to meet her head on would allow the matter to cease but her thought was short lived.

"Come now, Lady Adele. It is no secret the Lady Charlotte was brought up sheltered. Let us just be grateful she has basic comportment. It could be worse. I am surprised she is not out hunting in unique riding wear," tittered the spiteful tones of Portia. Charlotte heard some of the ladies laugh, which made her fume, as she was well aware several ladies had attended the modiste requesting something similar.

Emma, seeing she was becoming outnumbered, flew to her defence immediately.

"My friend is more a lady then both of you harpies

combined. Painting a watercolour with skill does not make you a lady, nor does it give you leave to be so rude."

Louise, who had been listening, content to let the ladies bicker and insult Charlotte, now intervened. She enjoyed nothing more than pulling her stepdaughter into line.

"Emma, how dare you speak that way to my guests? Apologise immediately or take yourself to your room."

"I believe I tire of your guests, so I am happy to depart." Emma stood up and took her leave but motioned for her friends to stay, wanting time alone to cool off. Charlotte whirled on Louise not caring she was the countess and the hostess. Why was polite society so rude!

"I think you took umbrage with the wrong person, Countess."

Louise's only response was to shrug. She cared little that she had upset Emma. Portia, not wanting to miss an opportunity to take a final shot, exclaimed loudly for everyone to hear. "It is no wonder the Marquess of Sunderland showers me with so much attention. He will need a true lady to be his future duchess."

Charlotte, shaking with fury, did not trust herself to respond and chose to walk away. Harriet and Eleanor looked at each other, having stayed silent in this exchange, being the quieter of their foursome. They jumped up to chase after Charlotte who they saw was stomping away in her strong, proud walk.

Adam stared up at the canopy of alder trees and sighed. *For the most part,* he thought, *everyone had been cordial.* They were all a part of the peerage and had run in the same or similar circles for years. The fox hunt had been arranged superbly. The Earl of Moreland had excellently trained fox hounds of impeccable breeding. They had also stumbled across some hares, so there was plenty of sport to go around and everyone was enjoying themselves. Sparing a glance at Jeremy and Anthony, he stifled his laughter. They were both sporting headaches after imbibing too much the night before. Jeremy had taken one of Louise's widowed guests to bed, so he had gotten little sleep on top of that. Lucas had not even bothered to come along with them, claiming he was unwell and wanted to rest so he could attend the evening's entertainment. *And me, I'm just in a foul mood,* he grumbled to himself. He had had a restless sleep, being tempted to sneak into Charlotte's room, and tossed and turned with indecision until his sense of decency won out. Now he was spending the day with her would be suitor. He cast a sideways glance at Sheffield.

They stopped for refreshment and the camaraderie of the hunt was put to the test. "Sheffield, I have seen you cosy up to Kentwell's chit this season, pray tell where it is leading?" asked Percy. "She is a real beauty; I hear she is a bit forthright, but I suppose she was indulged all those years alone at Kentwell," he continued.

Sheffield, noting Adam was following the conversation with a keen interest, responded with sly intent.

"Very perceptive of you, old fellow. Nothing official, but I am confident we have built a strong connection and she has given every encouragement she would be happy I seek out the duke for her hand."

Sheffield knew the last bit was a little risky, but he needed to create self-doubt for that cocky Langdon. Percy, oblivious to the tension emanating off Adam, turned to him.

"I have even seen you share a dance or two with this

chit. You better snap her up soon Sheffield before Langdon over here takes any innocence she has."

The other men all guffawed at the crude suggestion.

Before Adam could explode in a rage, Anthony intervened, familiar with his friend's temper.

"Sheffield, Percy, shut it. That is a lady you are talking about and, Sheffield, I think you presume too much. Less you look a fool, do not overstep."

Sheffield flushed with veiled warning but said nothing. He would just have to remain satisfied he had gotten under Langdon's skin.

Adam was furious. What he wanted to do was pummel bloody Sheffield. Sense was slowly returning and any actions like that would just cause a scandal and that was the last thing he wanted for Charlotte. Now calm, he stepped away with Anthony and Jeremy, shaking his head as he paced.

"You alright?" asked Jeremy.

"Yes."

"Are you going to punch Sheffield?" asked Anthony.

"Not today."

"Why are your fists clenched?"

Looking down, he saw that his fists were still indeed clenched. Releasing them, he turned to his friends and laughed.

"No woman has ever had this power over me; I feel like a caveman."

"Well, you were always the most barbaric out of the lot of us," joked Jeremy. "Come, let's finish the hunt and get back and rest before tonight. I am going to need it."

The ladies and lords squandered away the afternoon resting or napping as the servants prepared the ballroom for the masquerade. Louise had instructed the maids to slip a note under each door and hang a mask on the doorknobs of each guest's room. She felt this added more mystery for the masquerade, the masks a surprise. *Such delicious decadence in anonymity,* she thought slyly as she bathed. *Such a pleasurable evening ahead, it will be.*

Macy came to assist Charlotte to get ready and was the first to find the masks and the note. Macy hand them to her and, with a raised eyebrow, Charlotte read the note out loud.

Mystery is the spice of life. Don your mask and enjoy the night.

Shaking her head, she looked to Macy.

"The countess is truly something else."

Snorting, Macy replied, "That woman behaves like she is debutante at her first season. It is all just fun and games."

They eyed the mask, which was in fact quite beautiful. A gold demi mask with large gold and white feathers. The gold paint was shiny and sparkled when it caught the light.

"It's lucky we packed a gold gown, milady. Who would have guessed it would match the mask so beautifully."

"You are right, Macy. Though it's thanks to you. You are the one who picked out the gown." They settled in front of the dressing table so Macy could do her hair. She watched Macy create an intricate up do reminiscent of a Grecian goddess and she could not help but blush, remembering Adam comparing her naked body to Aphrodite.

"I wonder what mask Adam will be wearing?" she questioned out loud.

"Whatever it is, he will be quite handsome."

She wholly agreed he would but stayed silent, less her eagerness to see him was made obvious.

The ballroom at Ellesmere had been transformed into a dimly lit, shadowed, and mystical scene. Charlotte saw Louise had gone for an Arabian night's theme; sheer gold and purple drapes decorated the walls, glowing candles in golden lanterns. She noticed, as she drew closer to a group of ladies, that some of the chaperones who had attended appeared scandalised and kept their charges close. Louise and Adele stood in the middle of the room, their gowns daring with low bodices. Charlotte felt as if she was back at the Cyprian Ball. Emma and Charlotte's eyebrows raised at each other at the same time as if thinking the same thing. She watched one by one as the gentlemen arrived, and she picked out Adam straight away. His golden mane shone brightly in the candle lights and his broad shoulders were easily recognisable after she had explored the wide expanse herself. At the sight of the men arriving, she saw Louise signal for the musicians to play a livelier tune and bid the servants to bring out the food. Charlotte and Emma rolled her eyes at each other when they heard her make an announcement in her usual dramatic flair.

"Welcome to my masquerade, darlings. Let's eat, drink and dance till our heart's content."

Grimacing, Anthony looked around the room, turned to his friends and let out a low whistle.

"Now I don't know about you, but this seems a little improper. What is she thinking?"

Lucas took in the guests, fifty in total, and threw back his drink.

"I hope she has a card table set up. I am not in the mood for dancing," he said, his tone surly.

His friends noted his odd mood but did not ask questions. If something was wrong, Lucas would tell them. Adam had been eagerly searching for Charlotte and he knew, when his eyes settled on a golden goddess, he had found her. Before he could make his way over, Portia and her chaperone approached him.

"Good evening, my lord." She stared at him expectantly. Seeing there was no escape, he asked her for a dance, looking back at his grinning friends with a grimace.

Two hours or so passed and Adam and Charlotte found themselves together for one dance and minimal conversation. Unbeknown to them, Adele had been watching. Grabbing her maid, who had been flirting with one of the servants, she slipped her two notes.

"Have your new friend give this one to the Lady in the gold mask and this to the tall Lord in the black mask with the golden hair."

Louise had the servants all wearing white demi masks,

which helped to mask their plot. Adele, sashaying her hips, sauntered past Sheffield and whispered in his ear, "It's time."

Sheffield made his way to the garden, the agreed upon spot, easily located under a flowered arch. A few minutes later, Charlotte stepped through the arch and was shocked to find James and not Adam. He smiled.

"You received my note. I am so glad you came."

He could see the surprise written all over her face, and he knew she had assumed Adam had sent the note.

"Oh, yes. I was curious about the note. It just said meet in the garden through the arch. This is not proper though we should head back," she said cautiously, a sense of foreboding coming over her. He grabbed her hands and drew her close.

"Please stay for a minute. We never get any time alone."

She was so distracted by the situation and how to get herself out of it, she did not hear the footsteps approach, but Sheffield did. Before she could react, he lowered his head to hers and kissed her. Charlotte went still with shock, the foreign taste of another and not Adam distasteful. It was just at this moment that Adam came through the arch. His oath of outrage brought her out of her shock.

"What in damnation is going on here!" he yelled at Charlotte, his face suffused with rage.

Turning to Sheffield, he took a menacing step further.

"You're a dead man, Sheffield."

Seeing the violence on his face, she stepped between them.

"No, Adam. Please do not do that."

Misinterpreting her intentions to avoid a scene, he turned to her, his eyes emerald ice chips.

"You choose him over me?" his voice dangerously low.

Aghast he would even think that, she stuttered for an answer. She was only trying to avoid a scandal. How could he not see that? How could he doubt her heart?

"Have a care, Langdon. If you draw attention, it will ruin her," Sheffield reminded him with a wary eye on his fists.

Charlotte found her voice and pleadingly said, "Adam, this is just a misunderstanding. Let us go inside and talk. You must listen to me."

He felt crushed and empty, his soul destroyed by the events that had just unfolded, and he wanted none of it. No excuses and explanations. He had made a mistake. In the coldest tone he had ever heard his voice take, he stared into her violet eyes.

"I think not, my Lady. I wish you and your viscount all the best," and he walked away.

Charlotte let out a cry of distress and turned to Sheffield.

"What just happened?" she cried.

"You tell me. I thought we had something. I did not know you also held Langdon in such regard," Sheffield replied in the most self-righteous tone he could muster.

She did not bother to hold back her unladylike behaviour, turned to Sheffield without a word, and kneed him in the bollocks instead, cursing him before running off. She did not go back to the ballroom and headed straight for her room. She threw herself onto the bed and cried until she felt there was not an ounce of liquid in her body. One note had ruined her life.

Adam went back into the party and could only see Anthony. He told him he was leaving and would explain when he saw them next. He knew, if he did not get out of this place now, he would not be accountable for his actions. Never had he felt so betrayed and devastated. Freddy saw the black mood of his lord and quickly packed. It was not long before they were on their way and, as Adam stared into the darkness, he thought *what a fool I have been. I swear to never open my heart again.*

Chapter Eighteen

Macy had told Charlotte breakfast was being served late and she asked Macy to find Adam and give word she wanted to speak with him. She did not go down to eat with the others, having no stomach for food and just wanting to speak with Adam. She had looked at her face in the mirror and saw how red rimmed her eyes were, her face pale and drawn. She refused to show any weakness in front of the ladies of the ton downstairs. She had received another note from Sheffield wanting to explain but did not care to speak with him. And she felt no remorse at any physical pain she had caused. What gave him the right to send such a note, the damn fool! She only wanted to resolve things with Adam.

Macy came back advising she could not find Adam nor Freddy. Charlotte decided to just make her way to the carriage. Exiting the room, she came across Anthony and Jeremy in the hallway and said a prayer it was not any of the women. They may even know where Adam is.

"Excuse me, my lords, do you know where I might find Adam, um, I mean the marquess?" An uncomfortable silence followed as she saw them take in her pale, miserable face and then exchange an awkward look.

"Ah, he left, my lady. He left last night," Jeremy offered, his tone laden with sympathy.

How embarrassing. I am to be pitied, she thought despondently. Her voice, barely above a whisper, stammered "thank you" and walked away. Fighting back her tears because she could not believe he had left her, she quickly rushed outside to ensure she ran into no one else. She had opened her heart to him, her innocence, and in the blink of an eye he had wiped his hands of her.

Anthony and Jeremy felt sorry for Charlotte. And for Adam, having no idea what had gone wrong last night. They hated seeing women teary eyed.

"Come on," said Jeremy. "Let's find Lucas, get back to town, find Adam and then find out what the bloody hell is going on."

The men found Adam at Gentlemen Jack's, furiously sparring. When Adam saw his friends, he called it to a halt, realising his reprieve was over. Jeremy pulled out a flask, took a swig of the strong, bitter whiskey, and passed it around. They all sat down and waited for him to talk. He took a deep breath.

"I caught her in the garden with Sheffield. They were kissing." His friends all wore identical expressions of shock.

"Can't be," Lucas exclaimed, stunned with this information.

"Surely there is some kind of mistake?" asked Anthony.

"She came to find you in the morning and was devastated you had already left," offered Jeremy. Adam shook his head.

"Nay, my friends. She duped me. The signs were there. How many times did I see her cosying up to Sheffield?"

Despondent, he put his face in his hands, shaking his head.

"I simply cannot work out why she agreed to marry me. How am I going to explain this to my parents?" His friends nodded in sympathy, no one sure what to say.

Lifting his head, anger rippled across his features.

"I will never let a woman fool me again. First and last time. When the time comes that I need an heir, I will find a plain quiet lady who will do just that and let me be."

His friends could see now was not the time to get him to think rationally. Instead, it was time to rally behind him and make him forget his woes. Jeremy took charge.

"Right, chaps, here is what we will do. Penthurst is having an intimate gathering and Willoughby is having a card game over at his place, so why don't we stop in at both and make poor choices all round?"

Lucas and Anthony nodded their agreement, waiting for Adam's reply. Adam stood, attempting a cheerful grin, and replied, "nothing would suit me better than getting back to my old self."

Aunt Anne and Macy were worried about Charlotte. Her drawn, pale, tear-stained face was all they could focus on. Charlotte spoke not a word in the carriage to Macy and Emma. Nor had she said a word to Aunt Anne upon arriving home. *The duke was not in residence and thank goodness,* thought Anne, as one look at Charlotte's face and he would storm over to Portsmouth to end the betrothal. Not prepared to let Charlotte stay mute, she knocked on her door but did not wait to be invited in. Charlotte was curled up in a ball on her bed, hugging a pillow, staring emptily at the wall.

"Please tell me what's wrong, dearest."

Charlotte heard her Aunt's concerned tone and felt guilty for the worry she was causing.

"It is nothing, truly. I am just tired. Upset stomach. I just want to be alone."

Anne was silent for a few minutes before asking the question Charlotte did not want to hear.

"Did something happen with the marquess?"

Fighting back the tears, she whispered "No."

Knowing how proud her niece was, and despite her maternal urges to coddle, she only said, "Alright, dearest. I will let you rest," and placed a kiss on her forehead.

Charlotte waited for her Aunt to leave so she could let her tears fall. She felt like the biggest ninny behaving this way. But her heart felt truly broken. All she could see was Adam's face, shocked and betrayed. How he left without a word, not even a message, she could not understand. She did not know if they were still betrothed. What would she tell her father? What would he tell his parents? How could she look them in the face again? If anyone found out, no one would believe her side of the story and she would be ruined. Her thoughts turned to the viscount, anger starting to brew.

How dare he take such liberties! I admit to being kind and friendly, but never did I encourage him to do what he did. Damn that man to hell!

Sheffield was not in hell but felt close to it. The plans did not go at all accordingly. Getting Langdon in a rage? Yes. But Charlotte falling willingly into his arms? No. In fact, Charlotte made it quite clear she abhorred him. His bollocks still ached. Sighing with regret, he wished he had never gone along with Adele's devious plot.

Happy but confused, Adele had seen Adam stalk out in the middle of the night. She had heard reports that Charlotte looked miserable and, when she saw Sheffield, he appeared regretful. But she didn't know any of the details! *That fop Sheffield refuses to tell me anything! Well, I am still appeased,* she thought. The look on Langdon's face had been quite satisfying. *And, who knows,* she mused, *I may very well end up back in his bed consoling him,* and her mind turned wicked.

Weeks past whereby Adam moved about in a haze of drunkenness. He had not been with any women. For the first time in his life, he was heartily sick of them. He had visited his parents and simply told them he had decided he and Charlotte did not suit and refused to discuss the matter further. The duchess was outraged, and the duke restrained her, stating, "You must let them work this out themselves." She told her husband and himself she would allow them till the end of the season and that was all. Adam rolled his eyes, half in annoyance half in endearment. His mother was truly as tenacious as a terrier.

"You will come to terms with it, Mother, just like I will need to."

Charlotte stayed morose at home, going for early morning rides before London awoke and spending her days reading or gardening in solitude. Tonight would be her first evening back on the social scene. She had been exchanging correspondence only with her friends, not feeling up to guests, but had agreed to attend the opera with them tonight. They had kindly been advising people she was not well to explain her absence at events.

Her father, thankfully, did not press her and just asked her to answer one honest question.

"Did he do something I need to call him out for?"

"No, Father. I simply changed my mind. The betrothal is off."

All the time alone had turned her heartbreak into fury. She was furious with Adam for not giving her any common courtesy to discuss this with her, having no faith in her the way she did with him. She trusted him, despite his libertine past! She did nothing wrong, except foolishly mistake a note. And speaking of notes, the one she received from

Adam was still making her seethe with anger, feeling her hands clench into fists as the lines ran through her head.

Lady Charlotte, I seek to end our verbal betrothal. As it was not formalised, I will inform my parents and will leave it with you to inform your father. Regards, the Marquess of Sunderland.

Pompous, arrogant, heartless fool! Every word was a knife to her heart. His formal coldness made her wonder if she only imagined the passion and love they had felt that night. As Macy assisted in readying her, she looked in the mirror and saw her sad eyes stare back at her. *Damnation, I am being such a ninny!* She attempted a big smile in the mirror.

"Tis time I move on, Macy. He never deserved my love."

"Aye, milady, that he didn't. You will look simply stunning this evening."

She had decided to wear a silver gown tonight, the shimmery material soft and flowy. Her smile became less forced as she gazed at her reflection. She was ready to face the music.

The opera at Covent Garden tonight was being attended by most of the ton. Adam, taking a sideways glance at Portia, wondered again how he had got himself into this plight. Well, he knew, he just could not remember exactly. Ever since Charlotte's betrayal, the days and nights had passed in a blur. All he seemed to do was sleep and drink. Somehow, he had ended up at some event with Portia's father and allegedly committed to going along with them to the opera.

He insisted Lucas accompany him to draw attention away from him being a single suitor. And he was glad he had. *La Donna del Lago* by Rossini had drawn all the gossips and he did not need any rumours circulating he was courting Portia. The romantic opera, inspired by the works of Sir Walter Scott, also did not assist the romantic mood in the air. Catching her flirtatious smile, he returned a grim smile, wishing he could shout at her that this was not going to happen. A new arrival caught the attention of the crowd around him and, as he turned, he saw a vision in silver step outside a carriage. Instantly, his body reacted. It was Charlotte.

Charlotte, Emma, and Eleanor alighted from the carriage in awe of the crowd and the sights of the Royal Theatre Covent Garden. The fluted columns and dramatic statues were breathtaking works of architecture. It was Charlotte and Eleanor's first time and they gazed in awe.

"Such a shame Harriet could not attend. She is so creative and artsy; she would have loved this," exclaimed Eleanor.

"She would. We will just have to come back again!" Charlotte squeezed her arm excitedly. "Come along, girls," announced Aunt Anne, who was acting as chaperone.

Emma pulled on Charlotte's arm and whispered.

"Adam is here and he is staring at you."

She turned around and met his stare, hoping the glacial expression she was aiming for was accurate. She saw him blanch slightly and she turned around, satisfied it had had the desired impact.

"Let him look. I have nothing to say to him. I will not be played a fool again."

Emma nodded and threw Adam an angry glance.

The ladies moved to their box, reserved for Kentwell, and settled in. Shortly after, she saw him entering his own box and her stomach dropped. Why was Adam assisting Portia into a chair? Turning to Emma, she saw her friend's attention was also caught but, following her line of sight, her eyes were trained on Lucas, who had just handed Portia a drink. They looked at each other baffled.

Adam was still reeling from the frosty stare he had gotten from Charlotte. He knew she was hurt but damnation so was he! Still, he could not refrain from the pride he always felt when she showed her strength. He exchanged tortured looks with Lucas over the top of Portia's head. She seemed to think they both were interested in her and was being demanding upon them both. Adam wanted the opera to start so he could steal some glances of Charlotte while everyone was distracted. He did not think seeing her would physically hurt but it did. He was glad to see her in the company of her friends and not a suitor, especially not Sheffield. Portia, who had been watching him with narrowed eyes, began to speak in a snappish tone.

"So, Lady Charlotte has decided to grace the ton with her presence again. She has been ill the last few weeks or that was the supposed story. She is truly not very ladylike. Last I saw her she was leaving Ellesmere looking miserable."

The memory brought a smile to her face. Lucas witnessed the ferocious look on Adam's face and sent him a warning glance. Calming himself from the concern of her health, the guilt as the probable cause and the rage he felt at Portia's comment, he counted to ten before replying.

"Maybe she looked so miserable because she was sick."

Thankfully, before Portia could reply, the opera began and he was left alone to brood in silence and think over his confusion. In all his initial anger and efforts to forget about her duplicity, he had ignored his feelings deep down. He still loved her. Bitterly, he cast one more glance at her. Love is not strong enough for him to forget the sight of her kissing Sheffield.

Charlotte would have enjoyed the opera more if she was not so on edge from Adam's presence. The heavy maroon drapes were pulled back, allowing full view of their box, though it was dark with only the stage lit. She could feel his eyes boring into her but, at this distance, she could not make out whether it was in disgust or longing. Regardless, it was making her heart beat faster. She could hear it even over a high-pitched aria. And she could not help throwing her own furtive glances his way.

The opera came to an end and Anne ushered her charges out to avoid the crush. They made their way straight to the waiting footman to lead them to the Kentwell carriage. Anne was anxious to return home, knowing Kentwell had reservations about Charlotte undertaking a similar outing to that which he had lost his wife. Emma and Charlotte did not catch another glance of Lucas and Adam. Eleanor, oblivious to any turmoil, was chattering about her favourite scenes. Not wanting to bring the mood down, they joined in. Before she knew it, she was home in bed alone with her thoughts. A tear slipped down her cheek as she imagined that night had never happened and instead it was she who had attended the opera on Adam's arm.

Adam and Lucas farewelled Portia and her parents as soon as proper society manners allowed and headed to White's for a nightcap.

"Portia is awful, isn't she?" said Lucas, taking a long sip of his sherry. Adam nodded.

"Sorry, old friend. Being consistently in my cups led me to agree to that bloody offer. My thanks for coming with me," he said gratefully, patting Lucas on the shoulder.

"Was seeing Charlotte a shock?"

"I knew I would see her eventually, but it still felt ... I don't know. I just feel like I went a few rounds at Jack's." He paused before continuing.

"I feel guilty hearing she was not well. It is my fault, isn't it? I sent her that harsh note as well."

Lucas saw Adam's sad face and decided now may be a good time to raise this.

"I spoke with Lady Emma at a soirée, after hearing those rumours, and she confirmed Charlotte was sick but heartsick. Lady Emma herself is not very happy with you and thinks you should have sought an explanation."

"You never told me this! And I don't care what she thinks! I know what I saw!" Adam furiously replied. Lucas could not help but feel defensive over Emma.

"I did not mention it as you have been out of sorts. And do not take your ire out on Lady Emma!"

Adam looked over his glass at his friend, noting the protective expression on his face.

"Beware the spell of the bluestocking, my friend. With intelligence comes cunningness," Adam spat out bitterly. Lucas could see his friend was still not ready to let go of his anger and, with sympathy, patted him on the shoulder.

"What is meant to be will be, Adam. There is still hope yet that this can be worked out."

Not replying, Adam swallowed his drink and poured another.

Chapter Nineteen

Charlotte found herself genuinely sick a few days after the opera, not the heartsick malaise she had been suffering but physically ill. Heaving up the contents of her stomach was extremely unpleasant and this was the fourth morning in a row it had happened! She had not mentioned this to her father or Aunt, not wanting to be coddled after finally deciding she was going to stop being a ninny over Adam. *No matter how hard it was seeing him last night*, she thought sighing as she laid back in bed.

"Rise and shine, milady." Macy's cheerful voice broke through her dark mood, as she bustled into the room.

"I have risen, Macy, but I refuse to shine," she replied, turning her face into the pillow.

"What is the matter?" Macy cried, rushing over to the bed.

"Oh nothing, I was just ill again this morning. The nausea has still not subsided."

Macy, not knowing how to broach the topic, stared at her mistress.

"Ah, um, do not be upset. But, um, is it possible and

please tell me if it is none of my business. I do not mean to presume! I just want to be sure."

Exasperated, Charlotte cried, "Damnation, Macy. What is it?"

"Could you be with child, milady? When was your last monthly?"

Macy stood on edge waiting for a response but, after a few minutes had passed, it appeared Charlotte was frozen.

"Ah, milady," she queried with apprehension, "Are you alright?"

Charlotte moaned, "No, I am not alright."

Sitting up with her face in hands, she thought in despair, *How did I not realise this myself? And I thought I was clever.*

"I am carrying a babe. Adam's babe. What have I done?!"

Her last woman's time was almost 8 weeks ago! Stroking her hair as Charlotte began to cry, Macy could not think of any words to console her. Charlotte knew she needed help, but not yet from her family. She needed to tell her friends everything that had happened. She bid Macy to send urgent notes for the ladies to call upon Kent House as soon as possible.

No more than an hour later, Emma, Eleanor and Harriet arrived, concerned for Charlotte. Macy led them out to the garden to have tea and they saw Charlotte listlessly staring into the distance.

"Charlotte, what is wrong?" they exclaimed in unison.

Taking a steadying breath, Charlotte told them what had occurred at Hallend.

"You must speak with Adam and make him listen about Sheffield," said Harriet.

"I agree, and that damn rake will do the right thing by you. Even he would not be so poor of character," stated Emma fiercely.

"Come here. Let me give you a hug," Eleanor offered in empathy as she embraced Charlotte.

"He won't talk to me, and I cannot write this news in a note," wailed Charlotte. "Besides, I do not want to marry someone who has assumed so low of my person. Nor marry someone who will feel forced."

Her friends, rallying around her, imparted soothing words of comfort, reassuring her that this would work out. Sniffing, thinking how lucky she was, she turned to her friends.

"You truly do not judge me? I know my entry into society has been rocky. I am loud, opinionated, basically a hoyden. But giving my virginity before marriage is the worst thing a lady can do," she cried into her hands. "Portia and Adele are right. I am not a lady." Emma scoffed at the ridiculousness of this remark.

"There is nothing to judge! Firstly, he was your betrothed and, secondly, society's double standards have never sat well with me." Harriet and Eleanor echoed these same sentiments. She reached out to hug her friends. Her moment of self-doubt passed and Emma's next words gave her comfort.

"Sorry. I keep telling myself to stop behaving like a ninny," she sniffed.

Emma waved it off.

"However, since we know how the ton views these delicate matters, we all swear to not let this go any further," Emma declared. A plan formed in her mind, so she told Charlotte she had an idea and to trust her.

The soiree Emma, Harriet and Eleanor attended was a lavish affair filled with guests. The garden was lit with lanterns, the landscaped courtyard forming a part of the event, and they huddled outside. Emma's Aunt Clarice was acting as chaperone. Emma had specifically requested her presence knowing she had no diligence for the duty. Her stepmother was attending but she would be caught up in her social circle nor did Emma want her interference. Emma needed to get Lucas alone to discuss Adam and Charlotte. Harriet and Eleanor were to act as lookouts for when the opportunity presented itself. Thankfully, Emma thought, her friends asked no questions as to why she chose to seek out Lucas. They were all just focused on Charlotte's welfare. And as Eleanor had pointed out, it made sense because she found Anthony standoffish and snobbish and that, as a member of the peerage, he looked down on her for having no title. While Harriet found Jeremy cocky, and he seemed to enjoy flaunting his wealth, which she found distasteful.

They huddled together in the corner of the garden going over their plan.

"So, you are going to ask Lucas to dance. Will he not find that bold? It is not common etiquette for a lady to ask the gentleman," queried Eleanor. Emma shrugged it off.

"I need to ensure I get a moment to talk with him, and that is all I can think of. He was affable last I saw him."

Except for that night at the opera, she thought in annoyance, picturing Portia hanging off him.

"You will not mention the babe, right?" asked Harriet worriedly.

"No, I just need him to convince Adam to speak with Charlotte and she will need to decide what she tells him," Emma firmly stated.

Lucas was standing behind the hedges when he heard the ladies whispering and heard his name. He hushed Jeremy and Anthony. They had been sharing a flask of Jeremy's strong whiskey, having no taste for the watered-down spirits on offer. He heard the ladies say they were going to get some refreshment and turned to his friends.

"Snobbish? She may as well have called me a prig," Anthony said, insulted.

"I do not flaunt my wealth! But I admit to being cocky," Jeremy declared, only semi-insulted, as he wriggled his eyebrows. Lucas slapped the back of their heads, exasperated his friends were focusing on themselves.

"Did you not catch the most important part! Charlotte is with child!"

This sobered the group right up. This had the potential to ruin reputations, especially Charlotte's.

"What do we do?" Anthony looked to Lucas.

"I will find Emma before she finds me and find somewhere we can talk where no one will overhear."

"Will you tell her what we heard? What if the babe is Sheffield's?" Jeremy asked.

"No, impossible. I have seen Charlotte and Adam

together. They only have eyes for each other," Lucas said shaking his head.

"Plus, we know she spent time at Hallend, and we also know Adam."

Anthony and Jeremy could not fault this logic.

"I just have the gut feeling there is something more to what happened that night at Ellesmere," said Lucas to his friends as he walked off to find Emma.

Locating Emma was easy and, as he approached her, he scolded himself for feeling so nervous. Greeting and bowing to her friends and chaperone, he asked Emma for a spot on her dance card and, as luck would have it, the next dance was a waltz – an excuse to hold her close.

Emma, relieved she did not have to seek him out, wondered if she had manifested the moment as it had come about so easily. The waltz began not long after he approached her and, soon, she found herself being swept across the room in his strong arms. Lucas, trying to stick to the task at hand and not focus on how right Emma felt in his arms, stared intently at her, willing her to speak.

Finding her courage, Emma straightened her spine and spoke. Lucas held back a grin as he saw her do this. Even standing straight, she only came up to his shoulders.

"I need to discuss something with you. It is of the utmost importance."

"Of course, my lady, but not here, too many prying ears."

"I understand, my lord, but where?"

Not wanting to alarm her, he chose his words carefully. She eyed him curiously.

"I hope you do not misunderstand my intentions, but I think it is best we find somewhere alone in the garden. If it is important, I daresay we do not want to be overheard."

Her face blushing, she nodded.

"Of course, you are right. And, no misunderstanding, I know you are a gentleman."

The way she said this sounded more like an insult then a compliment and he thought over their exchanges the last few weeks, wondering if he had done something wrong. *Does she not know I hold her in the highest regard?* The dance came to an end, and he whispered for her to take her friends to the courtyard and wait for him.

Emma rushed over to her friends and quickly gave them the update. They took Aunt Clarice along with them to the garden. Attempting to be as inconspicuous as possible, she watched Lucas through lowered eyelids. Her eyes lifted with a start as she saw him and his friends approach.

"Good evening, ladies." Jeremy's deep voice greeted them all smoothly one by one. He even kissed everyone's hand and lingered for a few extra seconds on Harriet's, causing her face to redden. Anthony followed suit but seemed tense, greeting Eleanor with a stiff smile. Emma thanked her lucky stars Aunt Clarice was oblivious as usual. Jeremy was not aware of this as he turned his full charm on her Aunt in a hope to distract her. Emma hid her chuckle. Lucas caught Emma's eyes and gestured for her to follow him. The group, standing in a circle in front of where Emma and Lucas were positioned, gave them cover to slip away to the garden.

Emma and Lucas took a path through the garden that led deeper till the only light was the moonlight. The evening was warm, and the pleasant floral aroma of the gardens was nothing compared to the honeysuckle he could smell rolling off Emma. He wished he could pull her close and press his nose to her skin. Before she could speak, Lucas pulled her behind a large tree and placed a

finger to her lips. She heard voices over the loud thump of
her heart.

Adele could not ignore her curiosity any longer. That fop
Sheffield had not even deigned to answer her notes and was
conveniently not in residence when she called on him.
Seeing him here tonight, she gave him no choice but to
follow her into the gardens with a simply put, "You should
be kind to those who know your secrets." They were now
alone in the garden and he looked none too happy.

"What do you want, Adele?" Sheffield began with
unveiled dislike.

"You know what I want," she purred, undeterred by
his ire.

"I should never have listened to you. Charlotte
hates me."

"I know, darling, but why? The plan did not go accordingly but maybe I can fix it if you tell me." Sheffield scoffed
at her blatant lie.

"I will tell you but only so you leave me the hell alone.
Charlotte got the note you wrote and came to the meeting
spot in the garden. She saw it was me and not Langdon and
she was, of course, disappointed. I heard footsteps and knew
they would be Langdon's, assuming he got the other note, so
I grabbed her and kissed her." Sheffield surmised the sordid
events and now hoped he could leave but she grabbed
his arm.

"You have not finished. Tell me what happened next,"
she said, the excitement evident on her face. Disgusted at
the pleasure she was taking, he continued stiffly.

"Langdon saw. I thought he was going to rip me apart with his bare hands. Charlotte stepped in between us, as if to defend me, and Langdon saw that as the ultimate betrayal. He clearly thought she was there of her own volition. Charlotte was devastated."

He glared at Adele's gleeful expression. "You are an evil woman, to be sure."

"Come now, darling. You did not seem to mind us plotting with mutual pleasure."

"Events I truly regret. Now you know the sordid tale. I bid you good night."

Adele watched Sheffield stalk off and laughed to herself. *Men,* she thought, *so easy to manipulate. And the ones you can't, well, ruining their lives will have to do.* She relished the thought of Adam feeling like a fool, annoyed he had never bothered to seek her out all these weeks.

Emma and Lucas stared at each other in shock and fury. Their expressions thunderous and their fists clenched. Emma spoke first, spitting out the words in a furious tone.

"That foul woman!"

"She is the devil's spawn," Lucas said, between gritted teeth.

"So, it was all a trick? Playing with people's lives because she feels rejected?"

"I knew Adam should be mindful of her. And Sheffield, that absolute idiot, being led around by what's in his breeches!"

Realising the crude innuendo made in front of a lady, he quickly apologised. Emma waved it off.

"Aptly described. How dare he go along with Adele's nefarious schemes. Poor Charlotte has been heartbroken over this." Emma turned on Lucas, venting her frustration towards Adam now at him.

"And your friend never allowed Charlotte to explain! They were both tricked but the marquess has come off the biggest fool due to his arrogance and stubborn pride." She crossed her arms over her chest in a defiant pose. Lucas admired her feisty attitude but quickly defended Adam.

"Come now, Lady Emma. The man's pride was hurt. How was he meant to know? He did see them kissing."

"Did he not think it was weird that he also received a note?" she demanded.

Come to think of it, thought Lucas, Adam did not mention a note, but it would make sense why he also went to the same spot as Charlotte.

"The man's heart was crushed. Mayhap in all of that, he forgot?"

Emma's scowl was indicative of what she thought of his defence. Wanting to steer the conversation, he said, "What do you propose we do now and, before you speak, I will tell you I overheard you speaking with your friends. You wanted to convince me to talk to Adam. I also know about the babe."

Emma lost her fury and filled with dread. She felt as though she had betrayed Charlotte. Lucas saw her expression change and was quick to reassure her.

"Do not stress. Only I, Anthony and Jeremy heard. We will say nothing. He is our best friend. Let us plan how we will help them work this out."

Feeling calmer, Emma shared her plans, knowing Lucas would agree.

"Well, before we overheard those vultures, I wanted

you to convince Adam to speak to Charlotte so she could explain, hoping he would realise it was a misunderstanding and she was innocent of wrongdoing. However, considering what we heard, you must tell Adam the truth. He will surely see he was mistaken."

Lucas nodded, seeing the merit in the story but knowing how stubborn Adam was, he would need to be brought around.

"And about the babe?"

"I think that is for Charlotte to decide." Emma quickly countered. "And if their conversation does not go accordingly, she will not tell him."

Shaking his head, Lucas paced back and forth.

"I need to tell him. This will surely make him see reason. He takes his duty very seriously." Emma held back her scoff. "I promised we would tell no one."

The sight of Emma gnawing on her bottom lip, eyes wide and worried made Lucas soften.

"How about this? If Adam is quick to be convinced, I will say nothing, as surely they will reconcile. But if the stubborn oaf needs a push, I will tell him then and only then. A man has a right to know these things as well, Emma," he said softly.

Emma agreed, knowing what he said was fair.

"Let us tell the others."

Chapter Twenty

Lucas guided Emma back the way they had come and they slipped into their circle of friends unnoticed. Aunt Clarice had disappeared, so Lucas and Emma quickly filled in their friends on what they had overheard. The four of them forgot the awkward time they had just spent together trying to make conversation, all coming together in unanimous outrage.

"I am of a mind to go punch Sheffield in the face right now," Anthony said, his tone menacing.

"Do not fret. Our Charlotte kneed him somewhere he will soon not forget," Emma said acidly, causing all the men to wince.

"I wish I could say I am surprised, but I am not. Adele has had an agenda since the season began," Eleanor declared, with Harriet nodding in agreement.

"What do we do now, ladies and gents?" asked Jeremy looking around the group.

"I am going to meet with Adam and tell him what took place tonight and Lady Emma will do the same with Lady Charlotte."

"What about the babe?" whispered Anthony. Lucas and Emma looked at each other, he nodded for her to answer this one.

"For now, we say nothing. Lucas will play it by ear with Adam and I do not want to upset Charlotte if Adam knows but he does not come to her right away."

"I hear your friend is a stubborn oaf," she added wryly.

The group laughed, breaking the tension, and agreed to take part in the next quadrille to ensure they behaved normally the rest of the evening. Lucas led out Emma, Anthony led Eleanor and Jeremy led Harriet and they surprisingly enjoyed a wonderful evening together.

Charlotte received a note from Emma, advising she would be coming over to pick her up and go for a walk in Hyde Park. She knew this was going to be about Emma's plans and her stomach filled with nerves. Emma took her carriage to pick up Charlotte and Macy, Aunt Anne proclaiming her legs too old to be walking around the park. Charlotte and Emma, mindful of their maids in the carriage, spoke of trivial topics, but Emma could sense Charlotte's tension. They thankfully reached Hyde Park very quickly and Emma bid the maids walk behind them at a distance. Clad in morning dresses with matching parasols, Emma and Charlotte walked arm in arm. They looked the perfect model of well-bred young ladies, and she could not help but snort out loud. She looked up when she heard Emma clear her throat.

"I have two stories to tell you. One is something I overheard the second is one which hopefully will lead to a solution." She stayed silent, the nerves in her stomach somersaulting with anticipation and dread.

"I overheard Lady Adele and Viscount Sheffield who thought they were alone in the garden. It appears it was they who had concocted the ploy to send you and Adam notes so he would find you at an inopportune time in Sheffield's arms. From what I understood, jealousy was her motivation and Sheffield wanted you to transfer any romantic feelings to him."

Emma saw Charlotte's mouth thin and tighten, her usual pink lips now white in anger.

"What kind of lunacy is this? Curse them both to hell!" she hissed, alarming a bird nearby who squawked and flew away scared by the furious undertone that belied in her rage.

"I am sad to say, this does not surprise me. The ton is full of unscrupulous people such as they." She patted Charlotte's hand, trying to soothe her distress, and looked around furtively to ensure no one was watching them.

"Now the second part. The reason I overheard what I did was because I too was hidden in the garden, with the Earl of Chester. We had sought out privacy to speak of you and the marquess. The earl was also aghast at what we had heard and will relay all that was said to the marquess. He believes a reconcile between you both will soon follow."

Emma waited for her reaction. Charlotte was caught up in a whirlwind of emotion, struggling to find words about the decision she had been wrestling with.

"Putting aside wanting to call out Adele and Sheffield, I have thought on this. Adam did not truly love me for else he would not have turned his back on me. I am going to tell my father of the babe and retire to the country under a guise of illness and will return for a different season. Maid or not, my dowry will smooth over any misgivings. Or I may never marry. I care naught for this place. I will not be a weak-willed woman who relies on a man for her salvation."

Despite her words, her tone was laced with regret, sadness, and uncertainty that Emma could clearly hear.

"Do you still love him?" Emma asked in a serious tone, halting their steps to stare her directly in the face.

"Yes," she whispered, meeting Emma's eyes.

"I think you should let this play out. He may have some explanation and apology? One you can accept?" Emma offered, seeing the pain in Charlotte's eyes.

"What if the earl tells him but he still does not care?" Her tone fraught with trepidation.

Emma now knew she had no choice but to tell her the other part and prayed Charlotte did not hate her friends for their slip.

"There is a third part. I didn't want to upset you further or, more selfishly, have you angry at us, your friendship means the world to us."

She just stared at Emma, who was chewing her lip nervously. Tugging her arm to walk, she pulled Emma along. With the adrenaline racing through her, she needed to move.

"Do not be silly. I could never be angry or, if I was, it could never end our friendship. I know you ladies would never hurt me intentionally. Tell me."

Emma could not help but blurt it out.

"Eleanor, Harriet and I were discussing our plans after checking around us to ensure it was safe to speak. We huddled near a hedge, the garden had them everywhere, but we did not check behind. And Lucas, Anthony and Jeremy were there and overheard. You will not be able to keep this from him, Charlotte, and I do not say this in support of myself, but I do not think you truly want to let him go. Especially as you still love him."

Damnation, she thought in panic. *Adam may find out about the babe. Will he still reject me? Me and our babe?* Concerned with her silence, Emma began to fret and grabbed her hands.

"Oh, Charlotte, please speak to me. I am sorry. We all truly are. They will say nothing to no one. In fact, they all hope you and the marquess work things out."

Squeezing Emma's hands back, she smiled.

"Hush, I am not angry with you. Just contemplating what will happen next. Maybe this was all for the best. And I will find out truly what kind of man Adam is."

Lucas had called over at Adam's bachelor pad and was relieved to find him home. He could tell Adam was in a brooding mood as Freddy led him to the study. Adam was sitting at his desk staring into nothingness, a half empty glass beside him. He looked up and saw Lucas, bidding him sit down, happy for the distraction.

"What brings you here, old fellow? Freddy, bring a glass over for the earl."

Lucas accepted a drink, holding the cool crystal glass firm, wondering how to start off. Taking a sip, he hoped to get some liquid courage.

"I have some news."

Adam lifted an eyebrow at this statement.

"News? Are you getting married?"

Lucas, taken back, sputtered.

"What? God no!? Why would you say that?"

Adam shrugged. He had noticed the way Lucas made calf eyes every time Emma was around or mentioned. But the bastard he was, he would be too bitter right now to even wish him well.

"Why else do you look so serious?" he said, eying the stiff way Lucas was holding himself.

"It concerns you. I don't know how to start but here goes. Remember when I told you to watch out for Adele?" Adam nodded, unsure where this was going.

"I wish I had pressed it more upon you. It seems that what took place at Ellesmere that weekend was due to, uh, some twisted scheme Adele had to ruin your courtship with Charlotte. That coxcomb Sheffield was in on it as well."

Lucas waited for Adam to say something, his frame had turned rigid, his face pulled into hard lines and etched with fury. Giving Lucas a start, Adam jumped up and threw his glass at the wall. It shattered, the brandy dripping down the wall in dark rivulets. Freddy ran in the room, saw Adam's face, and ran back out.

"They did what?!" he yelled furious.

"They tricked you but, them aside, you need to reach out to Charlotte and sort things out. You have not been yourself, man. You miss her. Admit it!" stood Lucas, raising his hands in supplication.

Adam refused to admit anything, despite knowing he spoke true. But he was still hurt by what he had seen.

"But why was she kissing him? Why did she try to protect him from me?"

Lucas rolled his eyes. Adam could be so thick-skulled at times.

"He kissed her when he heard you coming. It was a trap. If you had started to wring the fool's neck that would have attracted the whole party! Do you not think she was trying to avoid a scandal?"

"Mayhap she was trying to avoid anyone learning of her true nature! I know what I saw!"

Lucas saw the set of his jaw, indicating Adam was not ready to relent. *Damnation, he did not have time to be stubborn, time was of the essence with a babe on the way.* Knowing this would be the only way to make Adam see sense, he sent a silent apology to Emma.

"Adam, my friend, listen to me. Charlotte is with child, your child. I have known you to be reckless and stubborn all your life, but you never shirk your duties. You need to do something." Adam looked as if Lucas had slapped him.

A babe? he asked himself in wonder. Turning to Lucas, he repeated it out loud.

"A babe? But how? And how do you know?" The words came out flustered and shocked. All his anger had fled.

"Yes, a babe. Anthony, Jeremy, and I know from Emma, Eleanor, and Harriet. We are all working together to help you both be together. Now think about Charlotte, how upset and alone she must feel."

"Is she alright? Did they tell you anything else?" Adam asked filled with concern. Satisfied, Lucas told him all he knew. Encouraged with Adam's concern, he asked his friend what his intentions were now, as time was ticking.

"I am going to marry her, of course. She is all I ever wanted."

His fury returned now that he pictured the two people who stood in his way.

"Marry her as soon as I get my hands on that bastard Sheffield and that whore Adele. I will have her shipped off abroad, so I never have to see her again!"

Lucas lifted his hands in a pacifying gesture.

"Forget about them. The best thing you can do is be happy and live well. Sheffield will surely stay out of your way and Adele will slink off once she knows it all failed. Going after them will just promote a scandal. You have a wife and babe to think about now."

Adam nodded slowly, his anger cooling, hearing the wisdom in his friend's words.

"You are a good friend, Lucas; I would have been at a loss with Charlotte this season if not for you. I love her with all my being. I could have lost her due to my stupid stubborn pride. You have stood by me the entire time." The two old friends shared a gruff hug. Rarely, if ever, had they shared such heartfelt words. Adam declared he was going to resolve this now and saddled Argo and rode off to his parents, Lucas in tow.

The Duke and Duchess of Portsmouth were sitting in the garden drinking tea when he came storming through, followed by Lucas. Adam's somewhat thunderous but excited face alarmed them both, the duchess spilling her tea. The duke jumped out of his chair in concern.

"Son, what is it?"

"Adele and Sheffield tricked Charlotte and I to tear us apart. Charlotte is with child, and I am going to marry her. She does not know. I am taking the family carriage to Gretna Green. Mother, I need you to arrange to have her brought here, then tell her father."

The words came out in a rush. Lucas stood by watching Adam's parents gaping in shock.

"Good grief, Adam. You impregnated, Lady Charlotte?" yelled his father.

"You allowed that strumpet to come between you?" shouted his mother.

"Do not worry about what has passed, just help me with how to move forward," Adam shouted back. His parents started to calm and looked at each other.

"Of course, we will help you, son. We love Charlotte. We will protect you, her and our future grandchild," his father confirmed gently, starting to warm to the idea, now the shock had passed.

"That we will," agreed the duchess, "and a romantic impromptu trip to Gretna Green can be easily arranged. Take the carriage. I will have a bag of clothing and necessities packed that Charlotte will need." Adam smiled in relief at his parents.

The duchess, overwhelmed with emotion, hugged her son.

"Everything is going to work out perfectly fine. You leave the rumour mill up to me. I think everyone will believe the overbearing duchess I am, wanting you to stave off a wedding for my own sake, that no one will be surprised you both hopped off to Gretna Green." Adam, Lucas and the duke laughed. The duchess had never made a truer statement.

An hour later, Emma received a note from Lucas.

I will call on you tomorrow. Perhaps we can go for a walk. I have news of great import to share with you. Your servant, Lucas.

Curious as to what had taken place, Emma looked forward to his call. But try as she may, she could not help the blush that stained her cheeks when she read how he had signed the letter.

Charlotte also received a note.

I would love for you to accompany me tomorrow for tea. You do not need to bring escort or chaperone; I will send my lady's maid. I have missed your company so please do not disappoint. Yours truly, Duchess of Portsmouth.

Sighing, she knew she could not refuse. The last thing she wanted was to hurt the feelings of the duchess. She probably wants to probe about what had happened with her and Adam. She was surprised she had not gotten this invite earlier. Pressing a hand to her lower stomach, she knew she had to learn to be strong, not just for herself but for her babe.

The Portsmouth carriage pulled up at Kent House and Charlotte was already waiting outside, too nervous to be inside sitting and waiting. Entering the carriage, she exchanged pleasantries with a matronly maid who supplied steady chatter all the way to Portsmouth House, which thankfully was not too far. She was surprised that when the carriage stopped, the maid jumped out, not waiting for her. She shrugged it off. Who was she to judge what was proper? But, as she moved towards the door, instead of a footman, she came face to face with Adam. His handsome face stared at her. Her breath caught as their eyes locked and the air in the carriage grew heavy. He gestured her to move back, sat on the seat opposite her and tapped his cane on the roof of the carriage. "Hello, Charlotte," he said, his voice husky with the longing he did not want to feel. "We are going on a small trip."

Chapter Twenty-One

The Portsmouth carriage, behemoth in size and affording all possible luxuries, could not make up for the sheer awkwardness and palpable tension that filled its interior. Adam and Charlotte tried to ignore the feelings that had sprung between them: longing for one another. It had been so long since they were alone. Charlotte was also grateful her morning sickness had abated; nausea would have only added more strain to their already volatile situation. They were still furious with each other, equally as stubborn, and refused to be the first to budge an inch. So instead, they both went on the offensive.

"Kidnapping? I suppose you will not reach peak rogue status without at least one kidnapping,"

she sniped at him, her hands folded under her shawl to hopefully hide the shaking that would betray the cool facade she was attempting.

"Ahh, I see you have not lost your shrewish tone. Once a shrew, always a shrew, I guess. Maybe I was right to call off the wedding."

Adam bit back but instantly regretted it, as he saw the hurt in her soulful violet eyes.

Cursing out loud, he ran his hand back through his hair. *This is not how I wanted this to begin*, he thought. Staring out the window, trying to bring some calm about, he spoke, softly this time, his tone contrite.

"Forgive me. I did not intend for cruel words. I am not kidnapping you. I have a plan to resolve our situation in the best manner possible," he turned and offered a tentative smile.

Intrigued but still feeling cautious, she offered a small smile back.

"Alright, I am listening. What is your plan?"

Sending a prayer of thanks that she was open to listening, he quickly blurted out his intentions, his usual suave manner lacking. *Surely, she will be glad about what I propose.*

"We are on our way to Gretna Green." He was wrong. She was not glad.

"Gretna Green!" she screeched, throwing her hands in the air, her shawl floating to the ground as she stared at him dumbfounded.

Even a sheltered upbringing did not mean she was unaware of the purpose of going to Gretna Green. Gretna Green was infamous. Couples in England crossed the border into Scotland where marriages were legally sanctioned at a blacksmith without parental consent and forgoing any need for ceremony. Adam had kidnapped her to marry her without even attempting to resolve their problems by talking first. Adam, feeling a little put out by the response, stared back at her equally dumbfounded. She looked horrified! Weeks ago, she was ecstatic to marry him. Is it possible she no longer wanted him?

Narrowing his eyes, Adam blurted out the first thing that popped out.

"You are carrying my child, are you not?"

Charlotte did not think it possible to have her heart break into pieces all over again seeing they had not yet been put back together.

In a small, sad voice, she said, "so that is what this is all about. The babe. Not us. You now know I never betrayed you with my affections, but it still means naught."

Charlotte could not help what followed and sat there weeping into her hands. Adam felt wretched, wanting to comfort her but doubted she would welcome his embrace. She was such a strong, spirited woman, and look what he had done to her. He struggled to think of the right words. He wanted to be honest but did not want to cause any more upset.

"That is not the only reason. I ... I have missed you. Lucas told me what happened, and I know it was a misunderstanding. We were tricked. But ...," he trailed off.

Sniffling, she waited a few seconds and asked in a shaky voice, "But, what?"

Hesitating at the sight of her tear-stained face, he debated again on how honest he could be. Sensing his indecision, she insisted he speak and speak truthful. Her tone was stronger and he saw a fire return to her eyes.

"We will not move forward if we are not honest with one another."

"Well, it is just that, Sheffield always seemed to be hanging off you, like he assumed he held your affection. It never looked like you discouraged him."

Charlotte was offended but heard the truth in his words, as she had also thought the same. Before conceding, she wanted to point out that Adam was not flawless in all of this. She stopped crying and blew her nose in her handkerchief.

"You seem to forget who construed this whole fiasco: your mistress."

"I would not say she was or is a mistress. She was just a dalliance who expected more than she was ever going to get. But you are right. For her part, I am sorry. The signs were there but I ignored them."

Thankful for this acknowledgment and apology, she offered her own.

"I too am sorry I did not dissuade Sheffield as I should have. Besides you, I suppose he was the only other man this season who did not mind me for me. I could share my opinions, discuss any topic without judgement. But I only saw him as a friend, though I knew he had an interest in me. I should have made it clearer to him."

Pausing, she looked at him now with narrowed eyes.

"And during this time apart, were there other women?"

He could not fault her asking and he answered in a firm, sure voice.

"No, Charlotte. Despite my anger, all my thoughts were always on you. There is only you."

He saw her face soften and moved over to her seat, finally feeling confident he could take her in his arms without being rebuffed. He tilted her head up and saw her gaze lower to his lips. With a strangled oath, he took her lips in a desperate kiss. Calming himself, he softened and eased away, the pulse in his neck beating rapidly. Charlotte settled in the comfort of his strong and warm embrace, the kiss having the opposite effect by calming her. He stroked her back and pressed kisses on the top of her head, bidding her to rest.

"Our journey will take a couple of days. We have lots of time to be reacquainted."

The next few days passed in a blur for Charlotte. They rode for hours on end, stopping to eat and refresh themselves, swapping the horses and spending two nights at inns, but in separate rooms. Adam was the perfect gentleman. They talked normally, and he was very excited about the babe. He was attentive and courteous. And this was what was bothering her! Her roguish, teasing, lustful Adam was nowhere in sight. No words of love. *Perhaps he no longer holds an attraction for me*, she thought, glumly picturing a loveless ton marriage.

Charlotte could not be more wrong. He was in hell. He was making an effort to go slow and not overwhelm her. He felt guilty for the stress he had caused, finding out she was carrying his child alone all because he could never show any self-control. Once they were married, he would kiss her as much as he liked, hold her whenever he wanted. The close proximity of the long carriage trip was torture, her scent of roses, her tempting face and soft body so close at hand. Something was missing though, the fire they had between them was there but doused with wariness. He wondered if she truly forgave him and if she still loved him. Watching her sleep, he took stock of the errors he had made, his impulsive anger that had kept them apart and cursed himself for being a foolish idiot.

They arrived in Gretna Green, and Adam wasted no time securing a room and a wedding service. It was the afternoon, enough time to get it over with so he could have Charlotte to himself, as his wife. They soon found themselves standing at the renowned blacksmith's anvil ready to say their vows, but Charlotte yelled out, "wait!" He asked the anvil priest to give them a moment. Looking at Charlotte, he saw her violet eyes turbulent with emotion. He asked in a calm, controlled voice, "What is the matter?" terrified she had changed her mind.

"Tell me how you feel, Adam? Do you truly want me as your wife? Will you love me again one day?" The anguish was clear in her voice as she stared at him desperate with longing.

"One day? I love you this day and for all my days. I never stopped loving you! As for wanting you, it has taken every ounce of control to not have you till you were my wife ... and what of you? Do you love me still?"

Her eyes filled with tears, happy ones this time, and she threw herself at him.

"Yes, Adam, yes. I never stopped. I never wanted anyone but you. I will always want you," she cried. He caught her lips in a fierce kiss, the fire between them no longer doused but burning hotter than even before.

Taking a step back, her hands in his, he called the anvil priest back in.

"Marry us," he announced, his devilish grin, that she loved, back on his face as his emerald eyes twinkled with joy. He stared back and saw her eyes shining with happy tears and she had never looked more beautiful. The blacksmith said his spiel, pronouncing them wed, with the clang of his hammer striking the anvil sealing the deal. They signed the marriage document and, just like that, they were wed. He grabbed her by the waist and spun her around as she giggled.

"We should have done this weeks ago and saved ourselves the heartache," Adam voiced as he brought her back to the ground.

"The heartache has only made us stronger, my love." Her reply caused his heart to swell with love, knowing this amazing lady was his.

They decided to forgo dinner in the dining room at the inn, having it sent to their room instead. Adam had ordered a bath and could not think of a better way to begin his wedding night with Charlotte. He had slipped out to speak with his footman and came back to the sight of her in the bath, her naked skin glistening. Charlotte started when she heard the door but, when she saw it was Adam, she just blushed and covered her breasts.

"Do not be shy, my love," he said, his grin wicked, "You know I'm not." He removed all his clothes and strutted over to the bath, bending over to kiss her. Indicating for her to move up, he slid into the bath behind her, his legs on either side, as he pulled her back against his chest. "Adam, what are you doing?" she asked in a breathless voice.

He took the rose scented soap and glided it down her arms.

"Just bathing with my wife," he said, kissing her neck, his soapy fingers tracing her already hardening nipples.

Before long, they had soapily lathered and rinsed each other off, her shyness forgotten as her passion flared. Adam assisted her up from the bath so they could dry each other. She noted even the friction of the drying cloth stimulated her passion and her senses fled. Following the drying cloth, Adam placed sensual kisses, basking in her breathy gasps. He ran his hands over the creamy skin of her shapely body, which he had sorely missed. He swept her up into his arms to lay her gently on the bed. He lifted himself over her, just taking the moment to appreciate her in all her naked glory. Reaching over, he caressed her breasts and drew a nipple into his mouth. He could feel her strain for more as she arched beneath him, and he moved to her other breast. Charlotte was being driven wild with lust, but she pushed her hands against his chest, drawing her fingernails down in an erotic caress.

"I want to explore you like you do to me," she said, gesturing for Adam to lay on his back. Straddling his hips, she bent over to place pepper kisses on his mouth, the strong line of his jaw, his earlobe, his neck. His sharp intake of breath was gratifying.

When she moved lower down his chest, her long unbound hair caressing his body, he had to reach for his self-control. She kissed and licked his nipples and traced a path down his stomach but stopped when she was close to the proof of his desire. She could tell how much Adam was enjoying her ministrations; his breathing was heavy and his stomach muscles kept clenching. But she wondered if he would enjoy if she kissed him the way he had kissed her down below. Adam had watched her indecision under hooded eyelids, sending a silent prayer she would continue. She aroused him like no other ever had. She grabbed him with her hands, stroking him like he had shown her before, and lowered her mouth to tentatively swirl her tongue around him. He swore an oath and told her how good it felt, and that was all the encouragement she needed as she took him in her mouth in earnest.

The pleasure was more then he could bear, and soon he lifted himself up to grab her hips and lowered her down on to him, her own arousal paving the way. In this position she could feel him deep inside her, making her feel so incredibly full and close to him. She arched her back and gasped in delight, her senses heightened from the sexual anticipation that had built inside her. "You feel so good, my love," he managed to say through clenched teeth, as he tried to reign in the urge to lose control. He encouraged her to move and Charlotte found a rhythm that drove them both wild. It was not long before he felt her tremors and her muscles tense. The only sound in the room was their heavy breathing. Waves of fulfillment cascaded through Charlotte's body as she cried out her release, collapsing in contentment on Adam. He grabbed her hips roughly, thrusting furiously as he lost control and met his own release, roaring his satisfaction.

Staring at him in the afterglow of their lovemaking, Charlotte traced the outline of his chiselled face, knowing, even when they were old and grey, this is how she would remember him. His eyes caught hers, sated and filled with tenderness.

"I love you, Charlotte." His voice was thick with emotion.

"And I love you, Adam," she said, her own voice choked.

"And I love our babe," he replied, stroking her stomach lovingly as the sheer weight of his new life washed over him happily.

The trip from Gretna Green back home went very quickly. They were so caught up in their renewed love that all they wanted to do was talk and make love and sleep in each other's arms. As they drew closer to Grosvenor Square, Charlotte's nerves returned. Adam had explained how his parents were instructed to inform her father of his intentions and convince him to not pursue if he became angry. His parents were delighted about the babe, and they were confident Kentwell would be as well, once his temper cooled. Arriving at Kent House, they saw a Portsmouth carriage, also the Moreland, Chester, and Whitby carriages. Charlotte's trepidation was starting to overwhelm her but, as soon as Adam took her hand in his, her courage returned. They entered the drawing room and saw their family and friends waiting. The ladies squealed with joy when they saw they were holding hands, their faces glowing with love. The men restrained themselves to cocky grins, pretending they too had not been waiting on eggshells. Charlotte saw her father and ran into his arms.

"I am sorry, father; I hope you are not furious."

Her father hugged her and then stared back at her, moisture in his eyes.

"Of course not, dearest. If you are happy, I am happy."

He turned to Adam, his expression now stern.

"She may be your wife, but she is still my daughter. Do not pull any more stunts like this."

"I would not dream of it, your grace. All I want is for Charlotte's happiness."

To Charlotte's joy, they shook hands amicably. The ladies all took their turns to swoop and shower Charlotte with hugs and kisses, and Aunt Anne and the duchess wept with joy. Adam's father and his friends were shaking his hand and slapping him on the back, making jokes at Adam's expense. Kentwell cleared his throat.

"We have some celebrating to do. Let's toast to the

Marquess and Marchioness of Sunderland and the future heirs to the Dukedoms of Kentwell and Portsmouth."

"Hear, hear," yelled the men.

Lucas pulled Adam aside.

"I had a little chat with Adele and recommended she make herself scarce. What do you know, she has decided to take a sojourn abroad."

"And Sheffield?" he enquired.

"I hear a rumour he looks to marry some chit who has had her sights on him. I think he realised he soared too close to the sun when it came to your Charlotte."

Satisfied and grateful, he shook Lucas's hand.

"You are the best of friends."

Surrounded by their family and friends, who were over-joyed for their happiness, Adam and Charlotte could not help but feel as if they were the luckiest people in the world. Placing his hand over her stomach, in constant awe they had made a babe, the marquess kissed his marchioness, pouring all his love into the soul-stirring moment.

"Thank you for loving me, flaws and all."

"No, my love, thank you for loving me, shrew and all."

Epilogue

Two years later ...

The Marquess and Marchioness of Sunderland, Adam and Charlotte Langdon, woke to peaceful silence as the sunshine filtered through the curtain of their bedroom. Adam laid on his side, cocooning Charlotte in his arms. As usual, they both slept naked and, as usual, being in such close proximity stirred their passions. Charlotte could feel Adam's hardened arousal pressing against her bottom as he kissed her neck and stroked her breast. Purring with contentment, she offered no resistance when Adam moved her leg to take her, reaching her arm up behind her to bring his head closer. They loved each other with the intimacy only true lovers have till they both found their climax together, suppressing their moans in each other's mouths. Laying in contentment, they spoke softly.

"Are you ready for the day ahead, my marchioness?"

"Of course, especially after that invigorating wakeup call."

Giggling, Charlotte untangled herself from Adam's embrace, got up to put her robe on and sat down at her dressing table. They shared the master bedroom, not being able to stand the idea of living in separate rooms, as so many of their married peers did.

Adam laid back, his arms crossed under his head, and watched with unadulterated adoration as Charlotte brushed her hair.

"I wonder if I have time for a bath before ..." A wail cut short her thoughts. A second wail followed and, within moments, the wails became a competition of who could cry the loudest.

"Our reprieve is finished," grinned Adam. "The young lords awaken. Another morning waking up like that and we will no doubt have a little lady joining in those cries."

Adam ducked as Charlotte threw a pillow.

Adam and Charlotte entered the adjoining room, which was now the temporary nursery. They each picked up a twin, future heirs to the Dukedoms of Kentwell and Portsmouth, Richard and Colin Langdon. The twins stopped wailing as soon as they were held by their parents, bestowing their cheeky little smiles upon them. Both boys had inherited the golden mane from their father but, as their eye colour had settled, only Richard had developed his father's emerald green eyes. Colin, who was already coming to be known as the cheekier of the two, had inherited his mother's striking violet eyes.

"Come on, boys," said Adam, taking Colin and Richard into his arms. "Let's allow your mother to attend her bath and I will attend your breakfast and get you ready for your big day." He leaned over to give Charlotte a kiss on the forehead.

"Do what you must. I have it from here and I have a little surprise to show you later."

Intrigued, Charlotte bathed and wondered what Adam had in store for her. She dressed with care and assistance from Macy. Today her cherubs were to be baptised, with their families and close friends in attendance, as well as the town folk. Charlotte took one last look at herself. She was wearing a cream gown, the sleeves had little lavender caps that matched the lavender silk sash around her waist. Macy had pinned her hair up but left soft, loose tendrils around her face. Pleased with her appearance, something she had not been concerned about since the babes had been born, Charlotte mused how nice it felt to feel pretty again. Ready to tackle the day, she met with the house staff to ensure everything was in order, greeted the minister who had come to perform the baptisms and prepared to meet her guests. But she had still not come across Adam and the twins. No sooner than she had thought it, they appeared, all dressed in their finest attire, the boys little miniatures of Adam in their formal wear. Her heart swelled with so much love she worried it might burst.

Adam, Charlotte, Richard, and Colin greeted their guests, who would stay the weekend, as they arrived one after the other. Duke Kentwell and Aunt Anne arrived at the same time as the Duke and Duchess of Portsmouth, causing much arguing as to who would hold who first. Emma, Eleanor and Harriet walked in together, cooing over the babes and hugging Charlotte with joy. Lucas, Anthony, and Jeremy came in after, slapped Adam on the back in congratulations and shook the little hand of each twin. The baptism was performed, everyone praising the twin's good behaviour. Emma stood holding Richard as godmother, with

Lucas as godfather. Anthony stood with Eleanor as they were named godparents for Colin, with Anthony looking surprisingly comfortable with a babe in his arms. The twins were blessed and a garden party followed. The entertainment purely centred around the twin's antics, but never had a group of adults been more obsessed.

Adam grabbed Charlotte's hand and pulled her away from the party.

"It is time for your surprise. Close your eyes."

Charlotte let Adam steer her away further than she had anticipated, and she wondered where he was taking her.

He stood still and held her close, turning her so her back was pressed against his front, and placed his own hand over her eyes.

"I have been keeping a secret. The side garden I informed you was under construction for another stable was not for a stable. I found myself incredibly lucky you were so side-tracked with the babes, you did not even ask me your usual 101 questions," he laughed softly, as she stood on his foot.

"This is your surprise, my beautiful wife, a beautiful garden I started to work on as soon as I knew I was going to marry you. I know this is a place that will always have a special meaning to you, and you have been missing them being away from your childhood home." As he lifted his hand from her eyes, Charlotte saw a beautiful rose garden, cultivated with such care and love. She saw a sea of roses in shades of white, pink, red and, of course, the violet shade she had never seen till he had gifted her with her first bunch. Tears stung her eyes, as she thought how lucky she was that the once most notorious rake was a sensitive, loving man underneath all that bluster. Turning to place her arms around his neck, she kissed him on the lips, whispering, "I love you, my Marquess of Roses."

The End

Also by Steffy Smith

Dear Reader,

Thank you for reading my first novel *A Marquess of Roses*! I assume this means you are a lover of historical romance, and you enjoy transcending to a different period in time, as do I.

An English Garden series will continue to follow Lady Emma, Lady Harriet and Miss Eleanor as they find love of their very own.

Join me in the journey Lady Emma Finley and Earl of Chester, Lucas Belmont embark on in an *Earl of Bluebells* which I am currently writing.

My next release will take you on an adventure through the Scottish Highlands so

To be kept informed of new releases, updates and most importantly of all to connect with any feedback or reviews please reach me on the following:

Website: https://steffysmithbooks.com/ (Sign up to mailing list)

Instagram: @steffysmithbooks

Being a new author, I also humbly ask you leave a review on Goodreads, Amazon, Kobo, Kindle – whichever platform you use or reach out direct.

I thank you in advance for your support & truly hope you enjoyed *A Marquess of Roses*!